1

Islands of Mythras

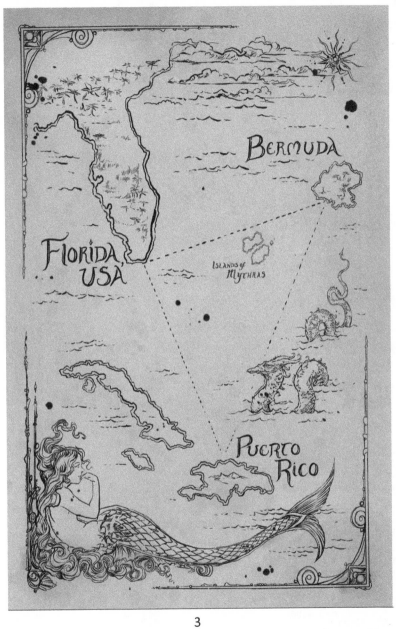

BERMUDA

FLORIDA, USA

ISLANDS of MYTHRAS

PUERTO RICO

A MARVEL of MAGICK:

Madden

and the Dark Unicorns of Danuk

By E.T. Page

Magick: (noun) The ability to cause changes to the conformity of matter or reality by one's will (not to be confused with 'magic', which is the imitation of magick by artificial means for entertainment purposes).

Felled bark and rotten branches broke violently beneath heavy, frantic cloven hooves. The sparkling one-horned animal resembling a horse was being trailed keenly by something dark, something large. A tempest flew from the colorless form, hurling into the night sky, tossing the treetops as they hissed and quivered. Galloping swiftly through the thicket, a pearlescent unicorn ran for its life.

Closer and closer the howling, cracking, crumbling sound approached, but other than the destruction left in its path, the tremendous power that followed remained indistinct. Strong, sleek legs pushed faster, harder, in an effort to elude the specter, but the violent shadow rushed behind, gaining ground.

With a quick turn, the unicorn thrust its robust frame to face the devouring void. The elegant four-legged creature stepped backward, paused and reared, its head and horn held high. Dazzling beams of colorful light began to emanate from its pointed spiral, illuminating the vastness of its uncanny adversary. The monstrous shadow stirred and hesitated against the flaring luminescence, yet it continued to advance.

Still facing the strange enemy, the unicorn withdrew a second step and reared again, aiming its spear-tipped weapon as more vibrant photons poured from it. Thundering shrieks and moans roared from the ghostly cloud as it pulsed, its size and shape fluctuating. Then it began to inflate and seeped forward, reaching out for the thing it desired.

With another quick turn, the unicorn jumped back into a gallop. The incredibly magickal creature was now being chased like a mortal animal.

What was this great dark devourer and where had it come from? What did it want? Unicorns were immortal and powerful, but they weren't invincible.

Continuing to push as fast as its hooves could carry it, the shining prey began to stumble and wane. Its legs slowed and buckled beneath it, as the insidious shadow loomed nigh. Aware of the terror that was nearly closing in, the unicorn finally came to a halt. It could move no further. With its last bit of strength, it lifted its head high once more, but this time only a dim glow flickered from the point on its forehead. The shadow was upon it now. Darkness encompassed the magickal being and absorbed it into its emptiness. Nothing was left. Nothing but destruction.

1

The Human Boy

Rain and wind bellowed briskly across the brick house at 906 Park Way. Thunder rolled across the sky, trailing just behind hypnotizing spectacles of lightning that danced over the dark night. Madden Edwards looked out through the foggy pane of his living room window as the show carried on.

"It's like magick," he said, still staring intently.

"Everything is magick and dreamland with you, dork." His older brother Martin's voice quickly brought him back to reality.

"Shut up, troglodyte! At least I use my brain," Madden jabbed back.

"Here we go again," Madden's younger sister Mindy said as she continued putting on a fashion show with her dolls.

Age-wise they were all spaced apart almost identically, with a four-year gap separating each of them. Mindy was a typical nine-year-old. She loved pink, did ballet with her friends, had way too many dolls, and swooned for every kitten she saw. Unfortunately, she was also allergic. Martin was tall and athletic, a complete sports jock and popular at school. At seventeen he always had one foot out the door, but still managed to find the joy in teasing his younger siblings.

Madden, being the middle child, suffered from all of the stereotypical ailments of middle children: overly insecure, a tad jealous, and always questioning his worth. He was small and thin. He was healthy, but still waiting on a growth spurt that was long overdue for thirteen. School was a bit of a different story for him. He wasn't very popular. He could get along with just about anyone, but really only had one good friend—blonde, sweet-hearted, and thick-bottomed Sienna Osborne. She had a sort of pre-indie goth chick thing going on, but it wasn't a big deal. Although she certainly leaned a little more toward the spooky things in life, she and Madden had bonded over a love of magick and witchy stuff. Having even a single ally in middle school could be the difference between surviving or not.

Madden's mother Melanie (the M names are not a mistake), brainy and beautiful, walked down the hall and into the living room. In her hand she carried a briefcase, and there was still a bit of spaghetti on her shirt from making dinner earlier in the evening. Her eyes were tired. She sat on the sofa next to Martin and resumed grading the worksheets she had assigned to her elementary school class.

Madden looked to his right at the blue book-bag he had used for the last three years. Seeing his mother grading papers reminded him of his own problems at school. He pulled the bag closer and slowly unzipped the largest compartment. Shuffling for a few seconds, he reached in and retrieved the folder that he had been avoiding all evening.

With stomach-churning reluctance, he opened the folder and pulled out his latest English test, which was marked with an intense red "D" at the very top. The son of a teacher, and he was doing worse than ever in school.

He looked over at his mother again. Her eyes were tired. He looked back at the test, where the "D" was still burning into the page. Just beneath it read, "Please have parent sign and return." Forging his mother's signature crossed his mind, but parent-teacher meetings were next week. Telling her would still be less trouble than he would get in for faking her signature. He took a breath and swallowed. There was really no good way to approach this.

"Mom, I just... wanted to tell you again how delicious dinner was tonight," he said.

"Oh thanks, honey. I guess I have my moments," his mom replied without looking up.

"And how grateful I am for you being such a terrific, understanding mother."

Melanie's pen came to a halt. Her eyes lifted from the pages of papers she was grading and met with Madden's.

"What happened?" She said.

He flashed a frail smiled that asked for mercy.

"I... need your signature on this. It won't happen again," he said.

Her eyes were tired *and* disappointed.

"What is this, Madden?" she asked with a sigh.

"I just... got distracted again. But Mrs. Bilmsbergh makes the English language feel like cognitive Kryptonite. She doesn't even like being a teacher. I think she must secretly be trying to bore her students to death," he said. He could faintly see his mother fight back a smirk.

"A 'D'? What are you, dumb?" Martin chimed in.

"Martin, please!" His mom scolded his brother then turned to him again. "Madden, we've talked about this before. You've got to focus when you're at school."

"I know, I try. I always start her brain-eating assignments right away. And then I start to... drift, and next thing I know I hear the bell."

"Nope, you're dumb," Martin said.

"Shut up, Ogre!" Madden shouted back.

"Yes, they are ruining our fashion show. Aren't they, Christie?" Mindy said, holding a brunette doll.

"Dumb-dee dum dum dum!" Martin continued.

"Quiet! Just quiet! For thirty minutes, I don't want to hear a peep! You know I had to work at the school and the bank again today, and I'm exhausted!" Melanie said before putting her face in her hands.

"Martin started it!" Madden said.

"No, I didn't! He's such a little baby! Wah-wah, baby girl!" Martin twisted his fists over his eyes to emphasize his taunt.

"Martin! Enough! Go to your room, both of you. Read and don't talk to each other for thirty minutes," Melanie ordered with a motherly authority that neither of them questioned.

Madden didn't like when his mom got upset. Especially when it was something he was responsible for. He and Martin were always at odds, typical for brothers around that age, and if Mom wasn't around to settle it, Martin usually did, being almost twice Madden's size.

Still glaring, the boys sulked back to the room they shared and didn't talk. This kind of punishment was no problem for Madden. He loved to read about faraway castles and magickal animals, beautiful maidens, and heroic princes. He loved all things enchanted, but there was one creature he almost always found himself drawing and daydreaming about.

He wasn't sure why. But why do any of us delight in the things that we do? Perhaps it was their power and strength that had always fascinated him. Resembling a horse, beautiful and sleek, with a single magick spear reaching from its forehead. Unis Cornu. One horn. The unicorn.

The stories about their adventurous journeys and valiant quests were far more exciting than Madden's algebra homework. It all seemed like so much more than fantasy when he began to read. There was something very real about it. And sometimes he found himself getting into trouble because of it.

Madden slipped into bed, and after reading a few chapters, he fell fast asleep.

His alarm sounded off like a threat, reminding him of his previous tardy record at school.

"Madden, come on, poopsie. You don't want to be late again," his mother's voice came from down the hall.

He stretched and rubbed his eyes and, after finally pulling himself out of bed, dressed and readied himself for school. Downstairs, his mother sipped coffee, and Martin and Mindy crunched on cereal while sitting around their kitchen table.

"Oof, we've got to go. You ready honey?" Melanie said

to Mindy, who nodded her head while she finished chewing. "You boys better hurry. Try not to be late today, okay?" Melanie gave a pleading look as she and Mindy headed out the door.

"Okay, Mom," Martin said with a smirk and then opened his mouth to show Madden his chewed cereal.

Madden faked a throwing-up motion and decided on an orange instead.

"Oh! Oh my!" Madden's mother's voice came from their driveway. He and Martin rushed out to see what was going on. As they made their way across the porch, something darted from under their car and crossed the lawn, climbing halfway up a tree. It paused as it reached the bright sunlight. It was a squirrel, but it looked hurt and sick, covered all over with some oily goo. After a screech and a shudder, it turned and ran back down the tree, into the shade and finally under a bush.

"What in the world? Stay away from it boys, it must have rabies. I'll call someone to have them come take a look. Now get going. I love you," Melanie said, heading back to their car.

The boys went back inside and continued to ready themselves. A few minutes later the chugging of the approaching high school bus could be faintly heard, which was Martin's cue to run out the door.

Madden ate quickly and headed out the door himself. If he took the road, the trek to his middle school was around a mile. If he crossed through the woods, it cut the distance almost in half. He couldn't be late again.

He walked down the sidewalk, passing several houses,

until the overgrown path through the dense trees slowly became visible and he headed toward it. As he stepped past the foliage, the early sunlight glistened through the forest, still damp with the night's dew. He continued on the trail for another ten minutes and then stopped and hesitated. After another moment of deliberation, he turned to the south, leaving the beaten trail behind. He made his way through the brush, and soon got a glimpse of what he had strayed for.

He continued until he stopped just in front of a very large twisted oak tree with several short wooden planks nailed to the trunk. At the top was a small dilapidated treehouse, set between four branches that made a perfect fit for the little compartment. It only had three remaining walls and the roof was half gone, but for the most part no one else paid it any attention. It was a place he could go to get away from everything else. As he began climbing the ladder he felt something inside his pocket. He fished the mystery item out and realized that he had forgotten about the Swiss army knife that was in his jeans from a few days earlier.

He finished climbing and pulled himself into the shabby structure. There wasn't much inside. Sunlight shined through the roof and single square window that was opposite the missing plywood wall. Several figurines were placed in battle poses next to a pile of others that lay on the floor. Madden stashed his pocketknife, knowing it had no business being at school, and quickly grabbed a few of his books, which were stacked on a small table in a corner of the room. He climbed back down and trotted the rest of the way to school.

After his first class, Madden headed through the halls of Washington Middle School toward his locker.

"Helloooo." Sienna's voice was a welcome morning energizer. "Where were you yesterday after class?"

"Hey, I... left a little early. Just to—"

"Yeah, I know, to avoid those halfwit jock idiots. You know if I'm around I'll stomp 'em before I ever let them tease you," she said, stamping her foot down.

Madden fought a grin and rolled his eyes. "Yeah, I know, and I love you for that, but I'm not exactly sure it helps my case having a girl defending me. But thank you."

They both laughed.

"Ha-ha. Alright, well, I still have to go to my locker. I'll see you in fifth period," Sienna finished with a hair flip.

"Have a nice nap with Mr. Eidelfouce," Madden said with a smirk. Sienna tilted her head back and stuck out her tongue while feigning a choking sound as she rounded the corner. Madden shook his head and again headed toward his own locker.

He entered his combination, and as he was fumbling through his books, he heard a familiar sound a few lockers down: the sound of a human body being shoved into hollow tin. CRASH.

"Oh, I'm sorry, nerd boy. Were you in my way? I think so." The brawny and handsome but despicable Tyson Oliver and his minions spread a reign of terror through the halls yet another day.

A smaller boy with dark hair began pulling himself and his belongings from the terrazzo floor. Madden looked at the boy who was so reminiscent of himself, and his heart sank. He was also aware that the threat was now coming his way.

Madden kept his head low and tried to be as

16

unnoticeable as possible behind his locker door, hearing the dreadful footsteps approaching. Closer... Closer...

"Sissy slap!" Tyson said, whacking Madden in the back of the head while he passed by. Madden put his hand up and ducked, anticipating further swings, but the boys had continued away from him. He had somehow slipped by with minimal damage this time. It didn't hurt too bad, really, but it made Madden angry and upset that these dolts could get away with this stuff. After Tyson and his henchmen had left the hall, Madden went and helped the boy gather his things. The boy seemed caught off guard.

"Jason, right? Tyson's a jerk. Don't worry about him. He lives a few houses away from me, so I understand. Just try and steer clear."

"Yeah, right. Um, thank you, really, but I... uh, I've got to get to class." The boy, still not quite together, turned and headed away quickly, dropping a pen on the way.

Madden, again simply trying to help, picked it up and called out to him.

"Ja—"

But before Madden could finish his name, the boy turned with a swift response. "Just because we have getting stuffed into lockers in common doesn't mean I want to hang out. It's nothing personal. I just... wouldn't want anyone to get the wrong idea. You know how it is already." He then saw the pen in Madden's hand.

"Umm, right... you dropped this." Embarrassed, Madden quickly handed him his pen and turned to head to class.

The rest of the academic day came and went, and as

Madden sat down in his final class he was pleasantly reminded of the current topic of study. He really did enjoy filling his head with new facts and knowledge of all sorts, but certain teaching styles, or the lack thereof, were what often made it difficult to regurgitate what his teachers required. History class and Mr. Jotson, who was his instructor, were on the good side of the teaching pendulum, and the history of the witch trials in Massachusetts was altogether a perfect subject for Madden to be wrapped with interest.

"In 1645 a mass hysteria started to spread throughout the state of Massachusetts, where some frightened puritan church goers were accusing and finding innocent men and women guilty under punishment of death for all kinds of reasons that today might seem silly, ending in 1693 in the small town of Salem. If you had an animal that you loved too closely, if you were a skilled healer, if your neighbor's crops didn't do so well, or if someone else had a bad dream about you, these things were all fair grounds to accuse you of what?" Mr. Jotson queried his class.

Glazed lackadaisical faces stared back without a hand going up. Madden subtly surveyed the room, and after a second, gathered the courage to raise his.

"Yes, Madden," Mrs. Jotson said, slightly surprised by whom the hand belonged to, and relieved that there was at least one raised.

"Of being a witch," Madden said. A few giggles came from around the class.

"Yes, that is exactly correct, Mr. Edwards," Mr. Jotson said. "If you all read the homework assignment you would know too."

"Most of the people killed had nothing to do with witchcraft," Madden added. "They weren't guilty. You could be accused for almost anything. And there were three books written by mentally deranged authors to help readers distinguish the signs of a witch. *The Malleus Maleficarum* by Heinrich Kramer, *The Compendium Maleficarum* by Francesco Guazzo, and *The Discovery of Witches* by Matthew Hopkins were all used to convict innocent people."

"Well that wasn't in the reading," Mr. Jotson said.

"I... did some of my own," Madden replied, "and if any of them actually were witches they wouldn't have gotten caught so easily. Not with magick." A brief look of puzzlement passed over Mr. Jotson's face, followed by a smile.

The lecture continued and the final bells tolled, releasing the students into freedom. Madden made plans for a movie hang out with Sienna later in the evening, and again left campus quickly to avoid the testosterone-infused brutes that attended his public school.

He headed home through the forest, reaching the pavement of his ordinary neighborhood street, and finally the patchy grass of his yard. He went inside and fell into bed, while his homework and what he and Sienna should watch later fought for dominance in his thoughts. He decided figuring out a good selection of movies would be a fine short break before he had to return to school work all over again. They had seen tons of the better fantasy and horror movies in existence already, and now were getting into the appreciation of the campy and genre originators. He went to the family computer and searched through some unfamiliar titles until he had come up with a few to offer and get approval of upon their meeting.

After his Internet surf he made himself a snack, and flipped around a few channels, settling on a classic cartoon while he ate, and then he started on his homework. His mother and Mindy walked in the door a half hour later, carrying bags of groceries.

"Hi, honey. Could you give us a hand?" Melanie asked.

"No, I shan't. You buy all the food in this house, and now you expect me to carry it all the way in from the driveway?" Madden said as he stood with a smile, walking out to join them in retrieving the remaining bags.

Melanie rolled her eyes with a chuckle. With groceries put away, she began making dinner.

Madden finished up his homework and thought it a good time to run his evening movie-hang desires by her. "So, Sienna invited me over for a movie. I thought I could go after dinner as long as I was home by nine. I've already finished my homework, and my history teacher was *very* impressed with me today," he said.

"Oh?" his mother replied.

"My extensive knowledge of the witch trials, *which* we are studying now. Not really a big deal."

"Well, that's wonderful, sweetheart. But I have some teacher meetings and I need you to stay home with Mindy until I get back. You might have to see a movie with Sienna tomorrow night."

"What about Martin?" Madden retorted.

"They have an away game tonight."

"Oh, well I guess his happiness is more important than mine. I get it, first born and all."

Melanie put down her cooking utensils and turned to look at him. "Don't be so dramatic, and don't forget about the

'D' you brought home just yesterday. I need some help tonight, okay?" she said.

Madden sighed. "Fine," he conceded.

"We can watch a movie," Mindy said.

Madden gave in and smiled. "Okay, kiddo," he responded.

He relayed his unwilling cancelation to Sienna, and they vowed to try again the next night. Then he slouched into a chair in the living room while Mindy went through a seemingly endless array of family friendly movie titles before they agreed upon one.

Sleeping Beauty was the settlement. It was a G-rating, yet had plenty of magick and thrills for Madden to enjoy too. But about halfway into it, Mindy squeaked and ran to the window that led to the side of the house.

"There's a horse outside!" she said.

Madden furrowed his brow as he looked over at her. "A what?" he said.

"A horse. I just saw it!" She said, craning her neck.

Madden unfolded himself from the chair and begrudgingly stepped over to see what she was looking at. He peered through the dark pane and saw nothing out of the ordinary in the dim light that was available. "I don't think so, buddy. Must have been a reflection from the TV," he reasoned.

"It wasn't a cartoon horse. It was a real horse, and it was looking in the window. I'm not crazy," Mindy shot back.

"Alright, alright. Well, I guess it's gone now. We'll keep an eye out for it," Madden said, snickering.

"Ugh, I know what I saw."

"Come on back and finish the movie. It's almost bedtime. It probably went to find some better grass than ours," Madden placated her.

Mindy grumbled a little more and then settled back onto the couch, glancing toward the window sporadically, just in case the horse she saw came back.

After the movie, Madden put Mindy to bed and began readying himself as his mother arrived home from her meetings.

When Melanie walked in, Mindy popped out of her room and repeated her story about what she saw out the window, swearing to its authenticity. Madden just shrugged and confirmed again that he hadn't seen anything, but they had watched a movie that had a horse in it. Melanie patted Mindy on the head, took her back to her room and tucked her in again. When she was sure the house was in safe order, she kissed Madden on his head, and they both went off to bed too.

The next morning Madden's alarm clock bellowed as usual, prying him from his sleep, and his routine began again. He hurriedly dressed and ate, before hurriedly making his way to school.

He went through the day, once more doing his best to slip past any of the threats presented by the crueler of the subspecies known as middle school teens, and started on his path home. Yet, as he found himself making his way through the wooded trails he decided to wander back to the solace of the little treehouse. When he arrived he crawled inside, curled up with a book, and couldn't keep himself from dozing off.

2

Beware

What You Wish For

Madden stirred as the sun was on the horizon. He exchanged a figurine, grabbed his pocketknife and climbed down from the treehouse. He started on his way back home when the distant crackle of snapping branches and the swift crunching of dry leaves rang out ahead of him. Something was moving quickly through the forest.

He looked about and listened carefully. What could it be? A deer? A panther? As it got closer, Madden caught glimpses of something shiny and white moving through the thickly woven flora. He saw the white figure darting through bush and brush but still wasn't sure what exactly it was or why it was so frantic. It also quickly registered, as the ripping sound thundered toward him, that he shouldn't stick around to find out.

He began to run back toward the path, but as the sound of the commotion drew near, Madden knew he didn't have a chance of making it at his speed. He took a sharp turn and slipped behind a large oak tree just as the chaos passed him. What he saw next left him breathless.

There, galloping in front of him, was fairy-tale fantasy come true. The pale animal was now in full view, but he could not believe his eyes. Four strong legs carried an elegant frame that seemed to move with a certain grace that mesmerized him—an awe-inspiring beauty that commanded his attention. Its coat seemed to shimmer like a brilliant snowy pearl, and upon its head the incredible animal was crowned with a single horn.

The young boy looked on in amazement and wiped at his eyes. It was still there. A unicorn. A real one. It had leapt right out of one of his dreams and into reality. But Madden's gaze was interrupted as he realized what was happening. The unicorn was in trouble. It was being followed closely by something obscene. Madden had been to the zoo and was an avid Animal Planet supporter. This *thing* was definitely not an ordinary creature. It was enormous, with a sinewy body that resembled a lion's but three or four times the size, its mass exceeding the frame of the sparkling unicorn. Its serpent's head stretched jaws that split open in four directions between lengths of fangs, exposing the folded coarse pink innards of its mouth as it screeched. The scaly head was attached to its hairy feline shoulders, where tremendous membranes of skin reached out over two batlike wings. It charged with keen talons on its front legs and cloven hooves on its hind, while a long crocodile tail whipped fiercely from its backside. A thick grey-black oily liquid covered its body, leaving bubbling slimy spills everywhere it stepped. Madden barely kept from heaving at the sight. The oily liquid reminded him of the mad squirrel he had seen the previous morning. As frightening as the beast was, its eyes frightened Madden even further. They were empty and vacant, and the glimpse he caught terrified him.

Madden felt himself panic. He wasn't sure what to do or if any of this was actually happening. But if it was, it was happening too fast for him to ponder any longer. Just above his head was a branch low and sturdy enough for him to jump up and get a grip on. He was scrawny, but his adrenaline made the climb to the higher branches quick. Not much further from the apparent danger, he looked back to see where the chase had continued.

He wanted to help, but how? What was going on? Had he bumped his head? Was this a dream? He stared down at the two animals as they now faced each other. The unicorn's head was held low, its horn shimmering. Its entire body seemed to shine as it took slow, daunted steps backward. With his mouth wide open, Madden couldn't move. He was wonderstruck and terrified.

As he watched with growing sorrow, an unfamiliar sound resonated through the air. He wasn't sure, but it seemed to come from the unicorn. The sound rang out again as the pearlescent animal reared, and this time Madden knew it had emerged from the shining creature. A moment later, he heard another rush of rustling through the thicket, only now it was coming from behind. Something else was approaching, and fast. He immediately feared the worst and thought he and the unicorn would surely be finished. As tears rolled down his face, he remembered his pocketknife and reached for it. Not much, he thought, but he would at least go out with a fight.

To his astonishment, the approaching sound was not

of another predator at all. A huge stag emerged from the thickness of the forest, adorned with a crown of antlers that was impressive to Madden even in the current situation. Charging at full speed, the great stag lowered its weapons and aimed them directly at the stomach and ribs of the hideous thing. It had come to help the unicorn, Madden realized.

The dark thing roared as it was caught off guard by the blow and flew several feet with the stag's antlers deeply embedded in its side. But the beastly monster reacted with speed. Madden only heard a quiet groan as the stag stepped away from its adversary. A moment later, the stag collapsed. With a swift, razor-sharp slash of the monster's claws, the stag's blood had been spilled.

Madden looked to the unicorn. Its shimmer turned into a glow that got brighter as the monster slowly rose to its feet again. The horrendous beast was injured, spilling blood of its own through the oily liquid, but it paid no further attention to the wounded stag. It was after the unicorn. Madden thought to stay motionless and without a sound. Perhaps they would both just pass him by and continue this enchanted chase somewhere that didn't feel as threatening to his own well being as this super-close encounter. But his heart wouldn't let him be silent. He couldn't just let it happen. He had been shown something extraordinary (or was dreaming deeply) and he had to try to do what he thought was right. Gripping his pocketknife in his sweat-drenched palm, Madden slowly pulled out the blade. He had thrown knives with his dad and brother over the summers. A pocketknife would be a terrible throw, but he had to try.

Just as the dark dripping beast started after the unicorn again, Madden closed one eye and took a deep breath. He focused on his incredible target. With only one chance to save the unicorn, he pulled his hand back and sent the red-and-silver knife flying toward the head of the enormous predator. He felt as though he could see every rotation of the soaring dagger. He concentrated on it carefully and begged it to stay swift toward its mark.

The great beast began to lunge for the glowing horselike creature right as the shining blade pierced its scaly neck just above its shoulder. The beast let out a ferocious cry and fell to the ground. It stirred for a few moments, writhing in the oily sludge that covered it, and then seemed to shrink. No, it was definitely shrinking. At half its original size, it lay motionless in a slimy grey-black pool on the forest floor.

Madden stared down from the branch in utter disbelief at what he beheld. The unicorn took a step forward, but Madden remained in place, still unsure of the attacker's state. He kept his eye on the monster's body for signs of movement, and as he did, the oily puddle surrounding the thing began to swell. The beast sank into the dark bubbling pool, and soon it had swallowed itself up. Only some oil-stained leaves and Madden's pocketknife remained where the beast had been.

To Madden's surprise, the unicorn looked right at him. It was beautiful. Upon its pearlescent coat Madden noticed a small silver patch over its chest shaped something like a star. It took a few steps closer to Madden, and then to his even greater surprise, it began to speak.

"Fear not. I will not harm thee," the unicorn said. Its voice had a low, smooth timbre that was both confident and kind, which matched appropriately with its majestic appearance.

Madden was stiff, his jaw hanging low. The unicorn then looked to the stag that lay motionless.

"There is still time," it said as it lowered its head and brought its horn just above the eyes of the antlered animal. A faint colorful spark flashed just at the tip of the alicorn. Slowly, the stag opened its eyes and lifted its head. Madden observed, astonished. The unicorn had healed it somehow. It was alive and its wounds were mended. It stood, looked at its surroundings and back at the unicorn. Lowering its head in what looked like a bow, it turned and made its way back into the thicket.

The unicorn now turned to Madden again. "My gratitude, young human. But... why didst thou help me and risk revealing thyself to that beast?" the poised creature asked. Madden was still shocked and shaken, but he cautiously shuffled down from the tree. He wasn't sure what to say, or if he could even speak.

"I... I just had to. That thing..."

The unicorn paused for a moment looking the boy over, and then stared deeply into his eyes. After another few moments, he told Madden to use his pocketknife one more time. Madden quickly retrieved it from where it lay. It was still slicked with some of the dark ooze, which seemed to harden on Madden's hand.

"Bring it close," the unicorn said. Its horn lit up again, and the ooze cracked away at once. "Take a strand of my mane. Weave it into thine own hair, and thou mayst have one wish of thy true desire. Consider carefully before thou makest thy wish, and choose wisely. Some things are not meant to be. But because thou helpedst me out of the good thou bearest inside, this bit of magick I give to thee." Madden, still trembling, did as he was told and cut a single strand of hair from the enchanted creature. "I have so many questions. Can I wish for anything? Are there more like you? Where will you go now?" Madden said.

"Forgive my haste, young human, but I am needed," the unicorn said as it raised its head, its neck arching beautifully, displaying the sleek build of its powerful muscles. "Choose thy wish wisely," the creature repeated. Lifting its entire frame straight up on its back legs, it reared and turned, jumping into a gallop.

Madden watched as the unicorn caught a glimmer of sunlight and became invisible in front of his eyes. He stood alone in the forest, holding a strand of pearl-white hair in one hand and his pocketknife in the other. There was no sound but that of the wind and the birds.

That evening, Madden sat in his room, still trying to process everything that had happened. He had again missed his plans with Sienna, but she would forgive him, and he made no mention of the day to his family, knowing how it would sound. Mindy's horse sighting also seemed all too possible now. Madden still wasn't exactly sure if he was on his way to the looney bin or if anything would actually happen at all, but he sat in front of his bedroom mirror and chose a few strands of hair above his eyebrows. He had learned to braid by helping his mom and sister fix their hair, so at least that part was no problem. He twisted the shimmering strand of pearl-white hair over, around and back again until it was fastened in place.

But when he had finished and it was time to make his wish, he hesitated. After what had happened in the forest, if what he had experienced was real, he knew he needed to think hard on what his wish should be. The unicorn's warning echoed through his thoughts. His amazement at the sight of the unicorn was still vividly etched in his mind. It was like a familiar figure he had been waiting for; the doe-like round eyes, the shining glow of the coat and mane, and the regal horn adorning its head that brought magick to the world. What would it be like to live as such a magickal creature?

Madden began to drift into thoughts of escaping to a magickal world. Perhaps that would be his wish. He would escape the painful taunting words and hateful hands of his regular life. He would show everyone, including himself, that he could be special, invaluable, and beautiful. He could leave it all behind for more of the real magick he had just experienced. He would no longer be a burden to his mother or be burdened by his brother. No more name-calling or toilet diving. Middle school would be a distant memory in his new life.

The warning of the unicorn flashed again in his mind: "Consider carefully, choose wisely." *I better make this good*, he thought. But after more drifting through visions of unicorns and magick, he still couldn't settle on a wish. He began feeling a bit of guilt for thinking only of himself. *My wish should help the world somehow*, he determined. He sat for several moments, looking in the mirror at the braided strand. After going through the day's incredible events again and slipping in and out of dreamy thoughts, he lay in bed feeling silly, and after another bit of questioning his sanity, he fell asleep.

His alarm rang out and called him back to consciousness. The excitement of the previous day swirled through his head, although now he was even less sure of what to think of it all. He glanced in the mirror. The few pieces of hair he had chosen were still twisted together, but there was no sign of the white strand. The fear that he had actually had a full-on vivid delusion crept up in his stomach. But unicorn or no unicorn, he still couldn't be late for school. He dressed, and as he walked into the kitchen, his mother and Mindy were already on their way out the door.

"I love you, honey. Have a great day, boys! We're running late, of course." The door closed behind them as Madden poured some cereal and tried to eat quickly.

"You better hurry if you don't want to be late," Martin said as he slurped down the last of his orange juice and grabbed his bag. Madden held his bowl to his face and sipped the last of the milk from his cereal. He grabbed his own bag and they both headed out the door.

Martin's bus was already pulling away. He ran after it, shouting and waving his arms, book-bag flailing behind him. After a fifty-yard sprint, it finally stopped so he could board. Madden laughed. He would be right on time as long as he walked straight to school. He started on his route, keeping a good pace, and decided to get a chapter in on his way. He often read while he walked. It made the time pass quickly and the whole walk altogether less boring.

Madden settled into his book, looking up every so often so as not to trip or walk straight into a tree. He happened to come upon a very fascinating few pages and forgot to look up for a few extra steps... and that's when it happened. SMACK! Right into Tyson Oliver, right in front of his house. Tyson also just happened to be finishing his Tang, which was now all over his shirt... and all over his jock friends.

It was a nightmare come true. It couldn't have been arranged any more terribly. Madden froze in horror. All he could think was that this was way too much excitement for two days and he was now officially going to die.

"You're going to die!" Tyson confirmed.

Madden made a run for it, heading for the path into the forest, and the boys followed quickly after him. He ran as fast as he could. A sharp left and a hurdled fence led him through a narrow alley and out into the foggy wood. Past the boundary of the forest and into the thicket, Madden raced to evade the young persecutors.

"Hey, queer!" yelled one boy.

Madden kept running. He dodged tree and bush as he pushed through the woods, until a thick root swept both of his feet out from under him. He tumbled to the ground. To his surprise, he wasn't hurt, but his pursuers were upon him.

Before he could get up, Tyson kicked his side and stood over him. "What are you going to do about it, little sissy? He's always drawing horses and unicorns and he plays with all the other little girls. But you're not a little girl, sissy boy!" Tyson said, glaring.

Madden felt a knot twisting from his stomach to his chest. This definitely wasn't good. Something was about to come out. He couldn't help it. He tried to hold it back, but he couldn't. His eyes filled with warm liquid that began to stream down his face. And once it started, it was like the dam holding the weight of his emotions had washed away completely. "No, I'm not! I'm not! You don't know anything! Why can't you just leave me alone?"

The knot in Madden's stomach began to grow. Something wasn't right, and it wasn't just his emotions. He still lay on the leaves and dirt of the forest floor when his body began to change. The knot grew to each of his limbs, rendering him motionless. Then, as if in a timed sequence, lightning struck and a swift wind began to blow through the canopy of great trees that surrounded the boys.

"Help me! Something must have happened when you kicked me! I can't move!" Madden pleaded.

"Nah, he's just faking so we'll leave," one of the boys said as he walked toward Madden, who was still cringing beneath them on the ground. But the knot in Madden's body began to turn into a tingle... and then a vibration... and then Madden saw light everywhere around him. Something was happening that he had never felt before, and after a few more moments, his very figure began to rearrange. Suddenly pale pearlescent hair sprouted from pores all over his body and a slender lump began to protrude from his lower back. It grew several feet, and a wisp of flowing pearlescent hair sprouted from the end. It looked like the tail of a lion.

"What the...?" The bullying brutes looked on in frightened astonishment as the shape of the young boy they had just assaulted began to transform.

Madden tried to stand and managed for a moment

before placing all four appendages on the ground. His plump lips and tapered nose seemed to elongate and merge, as the hair on his head grew and began to line the back of his neck, which also stretched several times in length. Great muscles inflated under his skin while his legs and arms shifted into robust forelegs and hindquarters, and his fingers and toes curled under into fists that became hard, cloven hooves. The last thing to emerge as his clothing fell in singed tatters was a single ivory-like horn that spiraled just above his large brown eyes and extended up toward the sky.

What had happened? How had it happened? Madden could barely think, but impressions of the previous day raced through his mind. *The wish?* But he hadn't made one. Not consciously, anyway. Still, the magick the unicorn had promised was real, and it was working. Not exactly the way he had thought it would, but it had happened. He was changed, transformed. His shape was no longer that of a human boy. He had become something completely different, something unreal.

A new surge of fear began to set in. His vision was blurred and he felt as though every bit of energy had been drained from his body. He saw the shapes and silhouettes of his aggressive classmates all around him, but at a distance now. He felt that these must be his last moments. His life was over, and he must be having a seriously massive delusion.

But a moment later, a spectacle of light as brilliant as fireworks erupted between two trees a few feet from where Madden stood. The light dimmed to a violet glow and grew large enough for a cloaked figure to emerge. The figure knelt under its hood for a few seconds before standing, turning toward the audience of dumbstruck brutish boys.

"Run... now," a calm assertive feminine voice came from the figure a half a second before a golf ball-sized sphere of violet light emerged and exploded at the boys' feet like a cherry bomb. The boys all complied and quickly fled the scene, scared but free of any harm. Then the figure slowly pulled its hood back to reveal a beautiful young girl with warm brown skin and thick hazelnut hair streaked with highlights of gold separated into two long braids. Her large eyes were specked with shards of green, brown and blue like a mesmerizing kaleidoscope.

When she turned to look at Madden, she seemed to be astounded by the sight, but she quickly regained her composure.

"We don't have a lot of time, and saying that your safety is important to a lot of people right now would be a little bit of an understatement. I can help you, if you come with me."

Her voice comforted Madden for some strange reason, and through his confusion, he tried to follow her. She turned and led him back the way she had come.

"Jump through. I'll be right behind you." She pointed toward the cluster of light from which she had sprung. "Quickly, before it becomes too weak!"

Madden struggled to keep himself balanced but stepped closer to the glowing passage. He paused and stared into the shining light. Then came a hard shove from behind. He lunged forward and soared into the illumination. Just before he closed his eyes, he saw the young girl follow him in, carrying a heap of his shredded clothing.

After all the commotion, Madden drifted and his

consciousness slipped away. In his slumber, he saw visions and memories of his family. He and his brother shared huge smiles as they watched their parents dance in a loving embrace. Then his parents stepped away from each other and paused.

Madden and Martin's young smiles subsided. His parents took another step away from each other, and then another and another until they were both gone from view.

3

Eloria

Madden awoke to sunlight creeping through a dense canopy of trees. He was lying on a cushion of large, soft leaves and feathers. He tried to lift his head, but something felt different, odd. He raised it slowly, and as he did he saw the horse-like body that it was attached to. Again, the feeling of alarm washed over him.

Holy... I must be dreaming. Those boys must have knocked me out. He thought about trying to pinch himself, but the realization that he no longer had hands only scared him more. He extended and stretched the four long legs that were covered in pale pearlescent hair, with cloven hooves at the bottom. He stared in disbelief as he watched these foreign limbs obey his commands. Placing his new legs underneath him, he pushed himself upward. Everything felt strange and off. His balance was unsure and his head felt far from his shoulders.

He looked around slowly at the unfamiliar land in which he had awoken. He was perched just above the base of a mountain, tucked in a wide cave with several great pillars standing at its opening. Far in the distance below, he saw the ocean. Inside the cave, a statue of a kneeling man with great outstretched wings growing from his back stood just beyond the pillars. In each hand, the statue held an item. In his left hand was what looked like the sun, and in his right hand, a crescent moon.

Sunlight speckled and pierced the foliage of enormous trees that covered the incline. Nothing but a few birds and insects seemed to be around.

Madden opened his mouth to speak, but only a shrill yelp escaped. He tried again, focusing hard on enunciating. "Hello?" came softly. "Hello!" rang out louder the second time.

"Halloooo," a reply came squawking down from a tree. Madden looked up and saw a macaw perched on a low branch, boasting radiant red, blue, and yellow feathers.

"Hello?" Madden said again.

"Halloooo," the bird repeated again.

"Did... did someone teach you that? Do... do you have a master somewhere, pretty bird?" The bird flew down to a closer perch.

"Pretty bird," the bird chirped. Madden let out a sigh, turned around and took a few unsure steps.

"I guess you're not going to be much help," he said as he looked about. Then another voice startled him from behind.

"Tico has his good attributes, but I don't think he'll be much help for what we have ahead of us." It was the girl who had pulled him through to wherever he was. She still seemed a bit impressed as she spoke. "It's so nice to finally meet you. It's incredible, really. I was told about this day, but... you never know the specifics of how or even if it's actually going to turn out. I mean, magick is a regular part of my life, and I still wasn't sure if we were going to be able to find you in time—or at all. But it's true, so far. He was right, you're here." She finally took a breath.

"Where... how... what is going on... exactly?" Madden managed after a pause.

She smiled. "I'm Knya, and you are in Eloria: one of the last communities of magick." She said the last part with a hint of pride. "I had to bring you here—and from the look of things, it was just in time. How did you come to be as you are? In this shape?" She stared with her wide eyes.

Madden stared back, puzzled. "Okay, it happened. I died. Those jerks killed me and now I'm dead. At least it's beautiful here." Madden sulked to himself.

"You're not dead, silly. If we have all the right elements, we can bend the energy just right to let us open a passage and end up in other places. That's how we got here. A passage was made so I could find you, and we came back through the opening, to Eloria. Although making passages has been difficult lately. Things get all jumbled. We were actually meant to return to the Oracle's yard, but we ended up here in my village, not far away."

"Eloria? The Oracle? Magick? This is all just... not real. I have heard of lucid dreams..." Madden said as he looked down at his new legs, still waiting for them to disappear.

"Eloria is located on the eastern side of the island of Mythras Major, which sits within the northern region of the area commonly known as the Bermuda Triangle. I'm sure you've heard stories."

40

"Is *this* place why so many people go missing when they pass through?" Madden asked, stepping away from her cautiously.

Knya giggled. "No. But we do get some serious weather around us sometimes. Mythras is hidden by old magick and myth, yes, but I assure you, this is real and we need you. The earth needs you." The new stranger looked at Madden with earnest, yearning eyes and he gave in.

"Okay... so why does the earth need *me*?" he finally asked.

She smiled. "Well... there are those that have the gift of foresight and are able to see visions of what may come to be, though nothing is ever certain. These are called the oracles, and there have been many. There is a prophecy that has been seen and foretold by the last five great oracles, all plagued by one vision in particular. All saw the vision many times and recorded it. Something about an ancient evil rising at the dawn of the new aeon, and an innocent being, a boy child in a form that is not his own but that of another pure and magickal creature, a unicorn, must be kept from this evil's reach. See where this is going?

"Me?"

"There is more to it, but these oracles were separated from one another and had no communication. We only discovered the other matching prophecies recently. Our Oracle, Omnicus, who lives here in Eloria, has seen this vision since he was a child. We must go and see him. I'm sure he's worried and wondering where we are. Follow me."

Knya turned and began walking into the cave, waving him forward with a hand motion. Madden reluctantly and clumsily took one step, and then another, and then another, trying to keep up. They proceeded into a large tunnel at the back of the cave that shallowed and turned as the ground beneath them changed from smooth-cut stones and became more coarse. The tunnel turned again and light shone far in the distance at an opening. They continued toward it, and as they passed out of the cavern, a brilliant forest unfolded around them. Sunlight punctured small holes in the splendid wild tapestry above, which was filled with plants, flowers and birds of every hue. Vines draped with beautiful blooms boasted incredible hanging displays from top to bottom.

The path led further down the mountain into an area where the forest thinned, revealing incredible homes and structures of adept architecture that appeared to nourish the nature in which they were built. Levels upon levels, the evidence of human designed intervention climbed and interwove with the natural heights of the timbers and foliage, all the way to the far aloft canopy. Madden turned in a circle as he eyed it all, his mouth slowly falling ajar with wonder before smiling. "Wow," he said, admiring the sight.

Several people greeted them, all in some state of awe. Some knelt, some cried. Madden felt a bit overwhelmed but greeted them anxiously. He thought he should express some gratitude for their kindness and apparent wonderment at being in his presence, but he wasn't exactly sure what to do. So he lifted one leg and bent another in as good a bow as he could manage.

Then the crowd parted down the middle as an espresso-skinned elderly man with long, wild white hair and curious symbols painted on his face limped slowly toward Madden. In his hands he carried a woven ring of colorful flowers. For a moment the man's eccentric appearance made Madden uneasy, but he quickly felt calmed as the man got closer. The white-haired man placed the flowers around Madden's neck and said something that he didn't understand. "In Lux! In Lux!" The man and the villagers all cheered and seemed to rejoice.

"He calls you 'The Light,'" Knya said. "The Oracle is not far from here, but we should begin on our way." Madden looked out over the hopeful, crying, rejoicing faces. His own feelings were not so optimistic. The weight of what was happening had only begun to sink in.

4

The Amber Elephant

Madden's body still felt new, unsettled. He was learning basic skills all over again. His hooves felt heavy and hard at first, but he slowly managed the simple task of placing one in front of the other. He and Knya plodded along a wide coquina-speckled trail that was nicely shaded by an assortment of tropical trees and brush. A cool breeze floated about the warm air this way and then that like a gentle tide through the forest.

As he walked, he began to feel a peculiar energy that started in his head and swirled down and all over his body. It felt incredible—warm and tingly and vivifying.

"I'm just going to... stretch my legs a little," Madden said. He began to walk faster and faster until his gait sped into a trot. With each step the impression grew. He couldn't sense anything negative in his body at all. It was something he had never experienced before. No pains, aches, or even the heaviness of supporting his own weight. His muscles didn't tire as they had when he was a boy. It was as though his mortality was being altered, or maybe it was leaving him altogether. He felt more alive than he ever had, and nothing was without some degree of intrigue.

Before he knew it, he was at a full gallop and his new companion was far behind him. He reared and pranced and felt the deliciousness of his new being. The energy flowing through him was invigorating. He felt he could almost pour it out if he wanted to. He was beginning to feel a new power.

As he trotted back to Knya's side, he saw his environment somewhat differently. There were faint combinations of different hues surrounding her and everything else. He blinked his large, brown eyes and began to notice everything around him seemed to have a shimmer, a sparkle. The colors of the foliage and flowers seemed extraordinary. He felt energy all around him. He felt the life of the forest all around him.

"I think I should tell you," Knya said, retwisting a braid, "the Oracle was born of... unnatural means. He is the result of experiments that humans conducted many years ago. But they had no idea what they had created."

"What do you mean? What did they create?" Madden asked.

"You'll see. Don't worry. He's a little eccentric, but you won't meet anyone sweeter... not to mention more hilarious."

As they rounded the base of a mountain, their destination came into view. A hundred yards up, carved into the side of the mountain, sat an exquisite castle constructed of light sandy stones with brown shingled spires and roofs. Sporadic flecks of seashell and quartz dotted the building, glittering softly when they caught the sun's rays, appearing at times as if the castle itself was lucent. Thick twisting wisteria vines stretched over the exterior in several places, covering some structures entirely with rich green leaves and violet blossoms. A single tower stood above the rest of the architecture, reaching into a canopy of mist. Large stairs—two or three times the average size—ascended from the base of the mountain to the monument.

"Why are these stairs so big?" Madden said.

"They are made to fit a wide range of beings. Humans were not the first in mind when these were built," Knya answered.

They started up the great steps to meet the one whose counsel they sought. When they reached the top, they were greeted by two large fierce looking figures adorned in razor-spiked, bladed armor. The sight of them pulled Madden from the bliss that had been surging through him. He recoiled and gasped.

"Oh, don't worry about them. They protect the fortress from anyone meaning harm. Just enchanted armor, but they won't pay us any mind," Knya explained as she motioned him along.

Madden timidly passed the figures, following her through two arched stone doorways and into a brilliant hall. It was huge. The architecture was precise and beautiful, with ornamental accents carved into pillars and moldings. Large diamond-shaped and round windows symmetrically lined the walls, letting sunlight pour inside. Tapestries that had the look of long-past antiquity hung between a few of them. Four fireplaces were set in the room—two on the right wall and two on the left—each with a few wooden chairs and a small table or two of books resting on top of different bohemian-looking rugs. Several incredible statues splayed in fierce positions also decorated the area. Madden noted what looked like a dragon, two unicorns, a few merpeople, pegasi, winged lions, winged humans, and a few regular-looking humans among the stone figures. Many gave the impression of battling one another, wearing stark terrified emotions upon their faces.

They walked on a stone pavement that echoed with each footstep. Madden made sure to take especially light steps so as not to make too much noise. At the end of the hall, a large mirror hung beside the archway that led to the next area.

Madden froze as he saw his new body completely for the first time. Knya stopped and let him have a moment. He took a few deep breaths and then turned this way and that, observing each detail and curve. Then he smiled. He was a cute little thing with an almost completely pearl-white coat, flecked with a few small sporadic golden-brown spots, seemingly where he had once had a freckle or a mole. His large eyes remained brown, and just above them a blaze of pearlescent gold encircled his fifteen-inch spiraled point. His shoulder-length mane matched his coat perfectly, as did the tuft of hair at the end of his tail. He wasn't very big as far as horses went and would have technically only been a pony, since he was around thirteen hands by horse measurements. But his round foalish features fit perfectly with his kind, curious demeanor. Knya smiled too.

They passed through another archway and into a corridor, emerging at the end of it to behold beautiful, lush green gardens on either side of the walkway. They continued through the garden, and the walkway split to curve around a stone structure that looked like a grand gazebo. As they rounded the curve, the path opened to a remarkable verdant yard with a view overlooking the mountain. A large circular fountain babbled in front of the gazebo, ornamented in the center with a statue of a centaur, a unicorn, a mermaid and a winged man, each with a waterspout flowing in a different position. The centaur poured from a bucket, the mermaid from a seashell, the winged man from a pouch and the unicorn from the tip of its horn. A serpent encompassed the entire edge of the pool. Further elaborate statues were placed periodically throughout the flora that garnished the grounds.

All of this was marvelous, but it was what was inside the stone building that halted Madden where he stood. Just beyond the large pillars that lined the circular layout, a huge amber-colored elephant wearing a robe with golden trim and raised collar sat merrily on a great throne fifteen feet high. The throne was also crafted of stone, with detailed carvings of different animals and vines etched intricately into the top and running up and down the sides. The elephant was talking very humanlike with two middle-aged human-looking beings, one male and one female. To Madden's surprise, as the elephant noticed them, he gave a loud and enthusiastic greeting.

"Oh my! Well, helloooo, hmm, hmm. We have been sooo concerned, so worried, but here you aaare! And loook at youuu!" The great amber elephant spoke very well. He had a certain excitement about him, and a sound similar to muffled trumpets accompanied his eccentric speech between phrases. Knya and Madden entered the gazebo and approached the stout figure.

"Are you both okay? Knya, what happened? I kept the passage open as best I could. It was only supposed to be a pass between here and there. Where were you taken? Hmmm?" the elephant Oracle asked, lifting his ears.

"I made it through to find him just fine, but when we both tried to return, we ended up in the outskirts of the village," Knya said.

The Oracle drooped his head a bit, with as much disappointment as his elephant face could show.

"It could have been worse. We were strong enough to get back to the island," Knya added.

The Oracle lifted his head and cleared his throat. "Hmm, yes I suppose you are right, my dear. But the muck is certainly swelling. The magick keeps getting more and more mixed up," he said to Knya and then turned to Madden. "Now, gooodnesss, I am so very pleased to meet you, my little one. I am Omnicus. They call me the Oracle, but I laugh when they do. Hmm, hmm. Sounds so dire. Well, we're reeallyyy excited you're heeere. Knya is a doll, isn't she?" Knya bowed in response. "A meal, please, for them both? Hmm, hmm." Omnicus motioned to the man and woman who stood beside him. They nodded and left the gazebo.

Madden was somewhat taken aback and gave Knya a confused look.

"I know, not exactly what you expected, hmmm?" the elephant said. "Well, I just try and enjoy myself and make the best of my time here. That's all we really have in this life—the life itself, right? I suppose you could then say it's only what I have *in* my life that makes it worth anything. And even then, we could say that life is all really how you look at it. Any way you put it, we all know what makes us happy and what makes us unhappy. But for some reason, so many can't seem to act upon this simple knowledge. Ah, you can lead a horse. Hmmm?" Omnicus finally paused. Madden remained attentive through his confusion. "It's Mason, right? No, no..." Omnicus rubbed his head a moment.

"Madden," Madden offered.

"Yeesss, I knowwww. Fear not, little one, hmm, hmmm. I have been looking for you, though my visions have been a bit off lately and I thought we would find you sooner. Come closerrr. Aren't you gorgeous, you sparkling little pony-corn. Just perrrfect, extraordinary. How exactly did you... uh... what caused your transformation? Was it spontaneous? Oh, or perhaps transforming is one of your natural gifts?" Omnicus said, tilting his head.

Madden thought through the events that had led up to his body being reshaped. Some of the details of the actual change were hazy, but he remembered running from the boys and being at least partly responsible for rescuing a unicorn from that dripping beast.

"There was another one... another unicorn... in a forest near where I live. It was being chased by something... like a huge slimy snake monster. A deer came, stabbed its antlers right into that thing, but the deer didn't survive. That's when I tried to help too. My pocketknife—it was all I had, but somehow it hit just right and saved us both. Or maybe it just made it easier for the unicorn to stop that thing. I don't know. Then it spoke, the unicorn I mean. It brought the deer back to life and gave me a piece of its own hair. It said it was a reward and to make a wish very wisely. But I went to bed that night and couldn't think of a wish. I just wanted it to be something that might be able to help people... and I admit, I wanted it to help me too. The next day, a few hours after sunrise, it happened. Then I woke up here," he said.

The Oracle seemed intrigued. "Well, this is certainly interesting, hmm. So many bits to place. No one, even within this community, has seen any unicorns for some time. And taking the form or illusion of a unicorn might not be too difficult, but to truly become a unicorn would require incredible power. Yet, another unicorn could accomplish the magick necessary for the transformation. When you said slimy, could you elaborate?"

"It looked like it was covered in dark grey chunky oil. It left spots on the grass where it stepped," Madden said.

"Well, that is troubling and must have been frightening to witness. What a series of events to have been through," Omnicus said. His elephant face frowned and then he continued, "Unfortunately, we don't have time to play, hmm hmm. I'm about to tell you... some things that might be hard to nibble. I know you aren't used to any of this, Mashen, so just try to follow along and ask questions if you have them. I looove questions. Hmm, well, I suppose I should start as simply as I can..."

The large amber elephant closed his eyes and sat motionless for several moments. He then opened his mouth slowly, small at first, and then much larger very quickly. A hard sneeze followed, with the pinched sound of flatulence erupting from his trunk.

"Excuse me, this long thing actually has more allergies than I know what to do with." He took a deep, full breath.

"Now... ehmm... throughout the universe, there is light and there is darkness. We live somewhere in between, dwelling mostly in the light and avoiding the darkness. It was a long time ago when this planet came into being. But there are legends of the universe before our world. Many point to an existence in which all of the energy of light was concentrated within a single form amidst the darkness. At some point the light fractured and was sent hurling into the great infinity of nothingness that surrounded it. Yet slowly, over eons of time, the atoms of light that stirred in space began to find one another and as they came close, they realized they rather enjoyed each other's company. They radiated and continued to gather until they had formed firmament, what we call matter. From this matter came the stuff of stars and solar systems and galaxies. Discoveries in science have also come to support this idea.

"From this matter came you and I and every living thing in existence. We are all children of the stars and made of the same atoms that gathered in the cosmos so long ago. This is the light and the energy of life. We all exude light even in the smallest amounts. We call it the power, the source or simply the energy, and it is what our magick and lives are composed of. Hmm, hmm.

"There is magick, and it is everywhere and all around us, even now. Even people where you come from use and witness it all the time. They're just too busy to notice most of the time, but almost everyone can become stronger in its application as they are cognitively elevated. Simply spending time in nature elevates these abilities. But some creatures are naturally aligned to harness the power and, with a little direction, they can gather greater amounts of energy to affect their surroundings. You are one of these creatures."

"You mean unicorns?" said Madden.

"I mean you, Madden. You have always had a

tremendous light around you. Always kind to the earth and animals, you have always enjoyed the trees of the forest and waves of the ocean. But unicorns also possess great power. You've become quite a combination. I have glimpsed you many times in many visions."

Madden stared in disbelief, his eyes wide.

"I've honestly always been... almost obsessed with magick and unicorns ever since I was small," Madden said.

"Is it any wonder now? You were meant to. And these visions have not only visited me. Several writings from the past have been found pointing to your emergence. The last Oracle to sit here wrote that even though she knew she would not see a day in your presence, she was moved when she awoke from the vision."

Madden was silent and then took a deep breath. "This just keeps getting bigger," he said. "I'm sorry, I'm really not trying to be rude or ungrateful. I'm just trying to get a grip on everything." Madden's hooves clopped on the stone floor as he slowly paced to and fro.

The welcoming excitement then left Omnicus's enormous face, and he turned to look toward the setting sun as it sank slowly beyond the horizon.

"Well, you still won't be caught all the way up when you do... because that was only the good part, hmm, hmm. But there is also another side. There is also the darkness, and the wicked things that dwell among it. It is what lies beyond the borders of our universe and seeps through it, trying to separate and extinguish the light. The very atoms that joined so long ago and brought about light, life, and love have been at war with the dark energy for as long as we know.

53

"There is also a dark story whispered through the forest in the darkest shadows. It says that as humans poison the planet and continue to grow cold, selfish, senseless, the dark energy will reach a critical point here on earth. I can feel it. It's becoming a reality. And although there are many who fight for good, who are kind hearted and well meaning, greed and corruption are rampant in humanity, to the point of endangering the very planet we live on. But there are evil ones among the magickal as well, trying to harness the dark energy for themselves, and there is one dark vision I have seen far more times than I would have liked to.

"That face. That terrible face. He is the one whose pact with evil threatens life as we know it. The one that we must defeat. Not man, nor beast exactly, but a species somewhere in between. When the visions came, I dug through my books. After searching for days, I finally came across what I was looking for. I saw what they were—what he is. Known to paleontologists as Denisova hominin, they evolved naturally many thousands of years ago, but they were thought to be extinct after flourishing during the Paleolithic era. They were a magickal people—peaceful, in line with nature and more technologically advanced than the Mesopotamians.

"Danuk Maz Otfa Ye is the name he was once called. It means 'gifted among the many' in their ancient language, and it seems he was looked upon with favor up to a point. But something turned him, opened him to darkness. Perhaps the darkness simply beckoned to him. So clouded, this vision, so murky. When he was discovered dealing in dark magick, there were others in his tribe that caused him to be driven away—or to sleep. I am not sure exactly why or when he returned, or what's enabled him to live beyond as he has. He is over twenty-six thousand years old and incredibly powerful. But he alone is not what troubles us.

"It is the evil, mad plan I see before him. As I said before, unicorns also possess great power. And somehow he's found a way to manipulate it. Ooooh, I just see so much malice. He's capturing them. Turning them demonic to do his bidding. Eight, I keep seeing and hearing eight. I think that's how many he wants. The madness. He could do unthinkable evil with that collective power. How he has managed to acquire any at all puzzles me. I wasn't even sure eight unicorns were still left in the world, although I admit I am ignorant to any real count. Not to mention that there isn't a magician on earth who could contend with a unicorn head to head, so to speak. One alone possibly rivals the power of ten master human magicians and the like, maybe more. He must have found some rare enchantment, or deceptive trickery that I can't imagine in order to be able to overcome them. But he... I feel he has nearly reached his dark objective. It cannot be fully realized or we would certainly be aware," Omnicus said. The amber elephant stared at the unicorn boy before him. "Madden, I'm sorry to say that he will seek you as one of them without doubt."

A shiver shot through Madden, apprehension awash in his eyes.

"Not to worry, my child, hmm, hmm. We will not let anything happen to you. I must tell, though, that I have glimpsed... the horror he wants to unleash. I believe he is in league with an even more powerful dark spirit from the outer realm. He wants to use the unicorn's energy to open a passage to the edges of existence. He wants to call upon this evil from the depths of our universe and bring it here to reshape the earth... with darkness.

"It is a powerful force as old as existence. There is some part of it that may be necessary, but when it swells, we must push back. For although we know there is a cosmic balance that must be maintained, even we don't completely understand everything. Perhaps we are not supposed to.

"We do know that this dark power is not to be used by the living or any children of light. It directly contradicts what we are, and it will inevitably consume us. If darkness grows out of equilibrium, all of life becomes at risk. Our souls can even be swallowed and separated by dark energy and fed upon. There are certainly dark things in our world, and these entities can influence us from their realms, but there are ancient laws and forces that keep these things from entering and consuming our world. Traces and minor entities do sometimes emerge through the cracks, as these evil things are always looking for... loopholes, in a manner. Ways to circumnavigate the laws, like using someone from earth to help grant access to our realm.

"But fret not, child—where the light shines, darkness cannot prevail. No, no, no! Hmm, hmm. Yet this is how, time and again, it makes its way into our civilizations. It is an extremely tempting poison and easy to become deceived and devoured by. Even governed by the ancient laws, it will always deceive the wielder. Danuk should know better. He thinks he can control it. Oh, the egos of some creatures, hmm," Omnicus said, shaking his head. "Do youuu have any questions?"

After a deep breath and a solemn pause, Madden responded. "How do we stop him?"

"Well, with the unicorns, he poses too great a threat. We cannot risk war or that kind of destruction. But there is a weapon: the Cosmite. Your safety is paramount so that Danuk may never use you as a means for evil, but we also need your help on this urgent expedition to put an end to his atrocity. A key must first be acquired in order to be able to access this great magickal weapon, and you'll have to join the quest to retrieve it. You won't be alone, but it won't be easy to retrieve. In order to get the key, you've got to go and see some folks that really don't want to be seen, hmm.

"The merpeople, once friends of man and animal, have almost left the surface completely and rarely communicate with any creature of the land. Man's desire for power has polluted so much and driven them deeper into the oceans. But there is one place that they most certainly still enjoy the beaches. Procuring any conversation and convincing them will be something of difficulty. I would not ask if I thought there were any other way, but you, standing in their presence, will certainly help get the point across. You're going to have to go to the Siren Sound and somehow get word to them. It is far below those shores where the key should still be hidden. The key must be brought from the depths before we attempt to reach this weapon.

"The Siren Sound is not far from Eloria. It's just on the western side of the island. Normally I would send you there with magick, but as I said, things aren't working as they should lately. Because the distance is not great, it will be safer to do this the old-fashioned way. Hmm, sorry to say. You can make it on foot from here in just a couple days. Traveling this way, off of any roads, you can also stay hidden, and concealment is of the utmost importance. The island is obscured by its location and old magick, so I believe the journey will be a safe one, as long as you go swiftly. We don't want a war. We don't want destruction.

"Once you have the key, return to Eloria. We'll concern ourselves with reaching the Cosmite as soon as the key is in our possession. I have sent for assistance from the remaining magickal communities of the world, and hope to have word from them soon." Omnicus paused. He saw that Madden was anxious, although he stood listening politely.

"Madden, this is your choice. You can accept the task or not," Omnicus added. "I know this is a lot to comprehend so quickly."

Madden was silent while he took deep breaths, his thoughts racing. "And what if I just want to be a boy again and go home? What then?" But even as he said the words, Madden knew that he couldn't turn back now.

"Well, if that is what you choose, you can spend just as much time looking for a way to transform yourself back into your human form. Even my magick wouldn't be strong enough alone, but the decision is up to you, hmm, hmm."

Madden sighed. He looked at his unicorn legs and back to the Oracle.

"Of course I'll help," he said.

"There's a hero," Omnicus said with an elephant smile. "As I mentioned you won't be alone. Knya, you are so important to this task. In his current shape, Madden will not be able to do things that you can, so you must protect him. Danuk may already be devising a way to obtain him, and that can never be allowed to happen. I am also sending another companion with you for further protection, as I will not be permitted to join you. Torque! Where are youuu, you crazy little dragosaur? Torque!"

"I am here, madam, sir," a small rainbow-colored winged reptile replied with a tinge of an old English accent as it flew to perch beside the Oracle.

"Don't you madam, sir me, you scaly mini. Torque will accompany you both and help you along the way. He is also familiar with the path to the Sound," Omnicus said.

Madden looked at the ferret-sized creature and wondered how he was further protection.

"Permitted... to join us?" Madden said.

"Correct. I cannot go with you, and the circumstances are a very long story for another time. But trust me in this too—if I could go with you, I would not hesitate for a moment to do so," Omnicus said. There was a hint of yearning about him. "And, while you are away, I will search through my literature to see if there is anything that might lead to a means of returning you to your former form, if that is what you wish when you return. Unfortunately, the situation has grown so precarious that haste is also imperative, and we cannot enjoy each other's company for long. It would be best to leave at first light, but until then, please make yourselves comfortable."

Between the short journey they had made from Knya's village earlier that day and the excitement of speaking with the Oracle detailing the incredible quest laid before them, they were all but exhausted. Madden still felt the vitality of his new body, but weariness had again started to catch up with it. They were shown into a dining area where the two humans from the gazebo, who Madden was informed were Omnicus's assistants named Tajre and Meirvot, had a meal prepared.

Madden was served various fruits and vegetables, a few he didn't recognize, but everything was exceptionally delicious. After they ate, they were each shown to quarters with plush cotton beds. Madden's bed was the size of a California king and very low to the ground. The bedframe was like the rest of the fortress's décor, and had a medieval regal gaudy quality to it. The mattress was soft, and it felt amazing to lie down. Madden closed his eyes, and let his body rest. A few moments later, he was deep in slumber.

Omnicus and Torque remained in the dining area and continued to discuss matters by firelight after their new visitors had retired to their sleeping quarters.

"I must say, I only joined your grand explanation to our guests near the ending. Did you tell the boy everything you saw? Who he may really be? What he may one day do to the world, considering we survive this mess?" Torque asked.

"Of course not. He mustn't know yet, and I'm sure he's scared enough as it is. I haven't even revealed his full importance in conquering the present threat. The time was not right, and perhaps he will not have to bear such a burden in the future, if we manage this victory in just the precise way."

"Yes, perhaps."

5

Something Twisted

In the morning, Knya and Torque woke Madden as lightly as they could.

"Madden..." Knya said softly. When he didn't stir, she gently touched his back and he opened his eyes—calmly at first, but as his vision sharpened, he gasped. He took a few deep breaths, gathering his acuity and regained his composure. Knya and Torque gave each other a look and let him take his time. It was all still there. It was no dream.

When they had readied themselves, they began their journey as planned. Knya brought along a sack stocked with several types of nuts and fruits, and a leather pouch filled with water. She also carried a separate satchel that held a few trinkets along with Torque. The odd trio headed off together toward the western end of the island where the Sound lay, in search of an elusive people who mostly dwelled beneath the sea.

The forest was thick and green all around them. Enormous boughs and hanging vines lined the small path they walked. For much of the day they were quiet, and as afternoon arrived, Madden still seemed to be working everything out. As they passed a dell of bizarrely shaped tree root knees, Knya reached for a plump pear from her sack.

"You're still wondering if this is all real, eh?" she asked.

"Huh? Sorry, I... I'm just... I'm fine. It is a lot to get my head around. I've never been important—well, I mean, like this important," Madden said.

Torque poked his head out of Knya's satchel. "Life can be spontaneous and unexpected at times. Not to mention scary," he said.

"It is a little scary," Madden replied.

"Well, we are here to help in any way we can. We are now guardians of the Earth, all of us," Torque said.

"That's what scares me.," Madden said, looking away.

"Don't you worry. So far so good," Knya said. She took a bite of the pear and reached for another, offering it to Madden.

"What did Omnicus mean when he said he wanted to come with us but he couldn't? He seemed a little... pressed when he talked about it," Madden said before noticing the juicy fruit.

"Mm-hmm. Oh, that," Torque said. "Well... he is a little sensitive about the subject, and I suppose rightfully so. Now, I would keep this between us, but it is true that he hasn't left the grounds of that fortress in over forty years, and goodness knows he'd like to. It's a curse, see? Very powerful. An old battle right here on Mythras. Hasn't been able to break it for all this time, although he's certainly tried everything he knows. He hasn't given up, and he has found some promising rituals, but he's yet to crack it. That's got to wear at you after a while, especially being as proficient in the craft as he is."

"Woah... A curse? Forty years?" Madden said with wide eyes.

"But, they were victorious and succeeded in banishing the bad guys," Knya said with a smile, again offering the pear to Madden.

Madden took a breath then accepted and took a bite. It was sweet and smooth and delicious. It calmed him a little as he listened to the wind through the forest. The harmony of the foliage was beautiful, and a bird chirped a melody that floated along the breeze. Madden was delighted at the sound. As he soaked it in, a slight low rumble crept up to accompany the symphony of leaves, pine thistles and chirping. It sounded like thunder... and it was getting closer. They all turned to listen.

"We should get off the path," Knya said.

As soon as the words left her lips, fear struck all of them. Something dark was coming down the trail and approaching fast. Striding nearer it became discernable—and the sight was unearthly. The four-legged creature was gruesome, warped and twisted, bearing chains and gaping wounds. Missing flesh from its sides revealed festering organs and bones protruding beneath the clanging thick metal rings.

From all over its body, it dripped liquid that looked like the same dark sludge Madden had seen before. Its eyes were almost invisible—vacant, empty and all but lifeless. The animal's head lowered as it drew closer, and something else became visible. Madden noticed a single horn reaching from the forehead of the dreadful creature. It was a unicorn. But it was nothing like the unicorn Madden had met in the forest or the one he had become.

"Run!" Torque's voice boomed and sent a shiver of fear through Madden's spine.

"Get on!" Madden said as he knelt on his forelimbs and motioned Knya to his back.

"Smart boy," Torque said, pulling the top of the satchel around his head like a helmet to brace for the ride. Knya quickly hopped on and pulled her cape tightly in front of her. Gripping Madden's mane firmly, she sat unsurely upon his withers and they were off.

Weaving in and out of trees and vines that grabbed their legs and hair, they raced from the ghoul. Above them, dark clouds formed from the clear skies and blotted out the sun. The gentle winds that had previously played through the forest sped up and turned violent. Madden hurdled a felled bough, and a thick branch snagged the fabric of the food sack. All of their rations were spilled. Torque turned to witness the phantom beast trample their fruits into the ground as it raced after them. "Good heavens!" he squawked.

All Madden could think was *how could this beast be a unicorn?* Surely this dark creature was something else.

The forest only got thicker as they galloped, trying to elude the danger that followed.

Knya reached for a pendant with a purple gem that was hidden under her shirt and began to speak quiet words that Madden didn't understand. As she did, Madden noticed the forest was not as abrasive. The trees and vines were no longer scratching them and impeding their speed. The foliage now seemed to shift and move, bending away, creating a path that

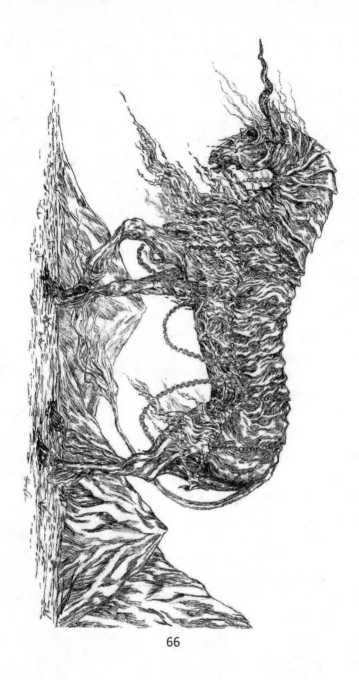

closed quickly behind them.

"It's gaining on us!" Torque called.

The frightened cry made Madden push harder when he thought he could not. Madden then began to hear strange whispers that seemed to come from nowhere and felt something tugging at him from all around the forest. He couldn't make out any words, but he knew it was calling to him. He began to feel faint. He slowed and his footing became unsure.

"Madden!" Knya screamed.

The terror in her voice reminded him of the evil that pursued. The boy who had become a unicorn regained his footing and darted forward again. Great oaks, ancient banyans and tallest kapoks now bent tremendously to make a clear path through the forest.

"Keep running!" Torque called again.

They galloped further amid the altering woods until they came to a narrow gorge. They raced forward, splashing through a shallow stream as the gorge continued to slim and its walls grew taller and taller. Passing through a final hedge of trees, they rounded a bend where the gorge ended abruptly at a great incline.

Madden shouted as he reared and placed his hooves on the sharp rocky wall, but it was too steep for him to climb. Knya's pendant was pulsing with a violet glow. She made a gesture and the foliage folded behind them, weaving a thick wall of tight bark and branches. They were trapped. They listened for any sound, anticipating the animal that followed. For a moment, there was nothing...

Then, just above the wall of flora, flashes of darkness erupted.

The winds strengthened, and the trees that protected them began to shift.

Knya quickly dismounted and etched a circle in the earth below her. She stepped inside, fell to her knees and began to draw symbols with her fingers. Torque opened his wings and flew from her satchel but stayed close. Knya continued and then shouted in the strange dialect that Madden could not understand. Three rings of violet light rose from around her and quickly flew toward the shifting trees.

"Madden, I need your help! It's too strong. You have the power. Concentrate. Call the energy. Focus. Use your magick!" she shouted.

"I... can't... I don't know how," he responded, but it floated away as a low whisper on the fierce wind.

"Focus! Try!" Knya pleaded.

Madden closed his eyes and lowered his head just a few degrees. It was so hard to concentrate through the fear and commotion. He remembered his quest to save the world and everyone in it. No pressure... and this was only the beginning. Flashes of his mother's warm smile and Sienna's laughter calmed him and gave him courage.

He looked back to Knya, using every last bit of her energy to protect them. Then he closed his eyes again and focused. He focused on love, on courage, on the boys at school that picked on him, on the wonderful new friends that were risking their lives for him.

The trees had all but come undone, and the ghoulish unicorn was again visible, prancing ominously between the great boughs.

"Grow," Madden spoke softly. "Grow, please." His

horn began to shimmer. "Help them grow," he pushed.

Colorful light swelled from the point on Madden's forehead. Knya's eyes lit up as she tried to stay focused.

"I knew it!" she shouted while new branches and twisting vines began sprouting from the foliage. The enormous shifting wall of trees slowly stretched and connected once more, but they would not be settled. "Keep trying!" Knya shouted again.

Suddenly, from the escarpment, a strange boy, who none of them recognized, swung down on a branch, soaring toward the demon unicorn with some kind of a sword in hand. With a swift and accurate thrust, the dark animal's horn was severed. The malevolent magick ceased. Knya and Madden let the trees settle and return to normal. The phantom unicorn writhed weakly as it lay on the forest floor.

They were all silent for a few moments, still amazed by what they had just witnessed. The strange boy stood by the now-stationary trunk of an oak tree, observing the dark beast on the ground. A puddle of oily liquid lay pooling and bubbling around the mangled creature. Slowly, the beast's body began to sink into the darkness, just as the strange chimeric monster Madden had witnessed before.

When there was nothing left but stained leaves and dirt, the unknown boy turned toward Knya, Madden and Torque. He had a slim, muscular build and stood about six feet. He wore tattered jeans, a thick woolen hooded shirt and a cloth pack on his back. His short sword hung in a scabbard around his shoulder. He removed his hood to reveal short espresso-brown hair and tan skin. He was handsome and looked to be around fifteen or sixteen years old.

Torque puffed a fire ring. "Careful of this one. He's got a hard look about him, and his blade cut through that alicorn like it was beechwood," he whispered.

"Definitely doesn't look like a local," Knya said as she slid a small blade of her own out of her boot and concealed it under her wrist. Madden made a mental note never to cross her. The boy stared at Madden for a moment, wide-eyed, and then began walking toward them. Madden lowered his horn.

"Don't be afraid. I only wanted to help. That thing, it seemed like it wanted to kill you. My name's Braelok. Lucky I happened to be walking close by," the boy said.

Knya looked him over for a moment. "Lucky? Who are you, and why are you so far out here in the forest?"

"Sorry, maybe lucky isn't the right word. I just meant... you're alive. Like I said, my name is Braelok, and I live in this forest. I was looking for food and heard screaming. In my understanding, someone should be grateful for being rescued."

"That... thing. Have you seen it before?" Knya continued.

"I've seen a lot of strange things lately. Animals getting sick, covered with that dark oily stuff. But it isn't oil. It's something else," the boy responded.

Knya took a deep breath. The boy was even more handsome up close, and they could now see his russet-umber gemstone eyes.

"Thank you... for helping us, Braelok, but we have to keep on our schedule and keep moving. Important business. Trust that, in time, you will be repaid for your good deed," Knya said, turning to walk away. She motioned to Madden and Torque with her head toward the mouth of the gorge, back the way they had come. Madden looked at the boy again curiously before following.

"Where are you heading?" Braelok stepped after them. "And in the company of a unicorn? I've never seen one, besides that dark thing that was chasing you. But I don't think that counts. I'm not sure that was a unicorn anymore at all," he said.

"Well, no time to share—thanks again. Have to be off now," Knya said as they continued, trying to hasten. Torque flew back to his place in Knya's satchel.

"Important business? Maybe I can help. I mean, more than I already have... remember?" Braelok said, following them with a big smile. "I can hunt."

"We don't eat meat—well, two of us don't," Knya said.

"I'm good luck," Braelok pressed playfully.

"We don't need it," she countered.

"I can fight. You almost got killed back there," Braelok said, sincerity rising through his jovial tone.

With that, Knya turned to face him. "Why are you trying to follow us?" she said.

Grinning, he responded. "What can I say? You're super cute, and it gets really lonely out here by myself. I'm reconsidering my life choices. And you keep company with unicorns. Must be good people."

Knya raised her eyebrow and crossed her arms as he continued.

"Listen, I was just on my way to a valley where I know there are *several* different fruits growing. Your sacks don't seem

71

to be too full. It's a bit hidden, but it's only another mile or so from here, and it won't put you off your direction hardly at all, whatever way that is. Let me show you, and if you want to be rid of me then, I swear I'll leave you alone."

Knya turned and they continued walking. She opened her satchel and looked at Torque, then patted her nearly empty torn food pouch. He gave her a nod and she did the same to Madden, who nodded in return. They stopped and Knya let out a sigh.

"Lead the way," she said.

"Now, see, that wasn't so hard, sunshine," Braelok said, still grinning, and took the lead.

They followed him slightly to the north, and after a mile or so, just as he had said, there was a valley with plentiful fruit trees. Bananas, pears and a few fruits unfamiliar to Madden dangled everywhere. Torque flew out and toasted a purple round melon before feasting. They ate a few and gathered all they could carry. Braelok filled his pack to the brim.

"Well, we've got to keep moving. This way is west... wait... right?" Through all the trees deep in the valley, Knya was finding it difficult to calculate directions. She turned in a circle a few times.

"That way is west," Braelok said, pointing. "I can help you make your way... and I can carry more food than you too." He smiled.

Madden looked at Knya after he plucked another delicious pear from a tree. "Knya... maybe... he could just... show us back to our path to get to the sea?" he suggested, chewing a mouthful.

"Oh, it talks! Whaaat?" Braelok said, observing Madden with surprise. "The sea, huh?"

Knya gave Madden a scolding look and took him and Torque aside. "Torque, you're supposed to be the Jiminy Cricket of this quest—what do we do?" she whispered.

"Well, my stomach feels much better, and I know I like him for that," Torque said. "I am perfectly capable of finding our way from here, but we still have much to do and far to go, and we're already exhausted. Perhaps we should give him a chance. His aid might come in handy. I am not a seer, but I do have some odd intuition that he is here for some purpose. But we shall all need to watch him closely."

They all camped in the valley, and throughout the night, mysterious sounds drifted upon the wind. Far away, beyond the islands and seas of Mythras, a fiendish, frightful cry ripped across the moonlight, bellowing from a dark cave, and an evil sentiment followed:

I will have you. . . Soon you will be mine.

6

The Siren Sound

A sweet resonance enticed Madden to wakefulness. The most alluring singing he had ever heard floated through the air and settled softly in his ears. He lifted his head to see where it was coming from. When his eyes had adjusted, he saw that Knya was the source of the soothing song. He noticed Torque enjoying the song as well, but Knya didn't seem to notice them as she picked a few morning blooms growing near the campsite. Free of the usual twin braids, her hair fell in tight cascading rings that nearly reached her waist. The sound, along with the morning sunlight glimmering on her face, was mesmerizing.

Braelok emerged and caught Knya's attention. She stopped singing and turned to notice them all gazing at her.

"Oh, sorry. I've always loved to sing, especially in the morning. My mother used to wake me with a song," she said.

"I'd love to hear that every time I wake up," Madden said. "That was absolutely beautiful. You should sing more often." He nudged her gently, and she smiled.

They gathered their things and set off again, deciding

to let their new companion, Braelok, join them, as he wished. After several miles, they noticed the forest began changing. They saw fewer and fewer oaks and more and more palms, birds of paradise, and finally sea grapes. The sediment slowly grew lighter and lighter too, until they were walking on a tropical sandy path.

"I think we should leave the trail from here. Travel just to the south of it until we reach the sea," Torque said. They did as he suggested and left the open path for the cover of the thicket.

"Do you think the merpeople will help us? They have to know something serious is going on by now. Maybe they've already started preparing," Knya said.

"I hope so, my dear," Torque replied.

"So that's why you're going to the sea? Merpeople?" Braelok asked.

For a second no one answered, and then Torque responded, "Yes. And getting an audience may be precarious. The merpeople have all but lost ties to the surface world. They were once great allies of man, but man destroyed their ancient alliance in his craving for profit and power. Overfishing and pollution have led to many battles and deaths on both sides. So many humans want to own everything."

"That's awful. Maybe we can help the old alliance. Maybe this... quest can, I mean," Madden said.

"It's a splendid thought," Torque replied.

"I can't believe we're actually going to see them. What are they like? Other than part fish," Madden said. He had always liked to read about merpeople too. He was almost as fascinated by them as he was by unicorns.

"They're not very different from humans in their basic social aspects. One thing that is certainly different is that they have not lost touch with the natural world, unlike so many in humanity," Torque explained.

When the sun began its afternoon descent, they began to hear the whispers of the sea. They pushed through the flora, toward the distant ruckus of crashing waves, and saw a cliff ahead. They walked to the edge and knelt to look at the inlet below. About sixty feet down, the ocean was a vibrant clear blue, glittering as it lunged forward onto the shores and sank away again and again. To their left, half a mile from where they stood, water from a brook fell to the rocky beach below, casting a glinting rainbow mist that drifted about the gentle sea breeze. They had reached the Sound.

As they admired the view, they noticed something else. There, sunbathing on the beach, were two creatures almost exactly as Madden had imagined them, only a little older and plumper. If Madden had to guess, he would have said they were in their seventies, but he wasn't exactly sure if aging was the same for merpeople. The closer of the two appeared male and had a husky build with copper-brown skin. The other was female and quite round with a deep olive skin tone. Their inhuman parts, although a bit tattered and aged, still had Madden in awe. Just below the thick bellies of the merpeople, sleek fishlike tails boasting shimmering scales, and fantastic fanning fins dipped into the coming and going of the sea. They seemed to be communicating in a unique vocal pattern unlike any Madden had ever heard. There were sporadic tones that had qualities close to that of an orca, only sweeter and deeper, yet there was a definite array of inflections that were apparent of advanced language. But after just a few moments,

77

the mermaid began slapping her tail and shouting at her companion, giving the impression that they were starting to quarrel.

"I think we'll pass on trying to speak with them. Looks like a lovers' dispute that we'd be wise to avoid," Knya said with a giggle.

"It also bears mentioning that the elders of some communities, although surely wise in many ways, are often the most resistant to new things. Like the idea of merpeople helping a band of strangers," Torque said.

"We'll keep looking and hopefully find someone a bit younger and in a better mood," Knya said. She moved forward without a sound, and the rest of them followed.

They walked along the ridge and passed over the brook, which was rather shallow but wider than they had imagined. It had plenty of rocks emerging from it to cross upon, and where the questing pedestrians intersected it was only knee-deep at its most treacherous point.

After another few hundred feet, Braelok spotted something else on the beach in the distance. As they approached, they were able to make out a much younger group of merfolk. There were three of them. They looked to be teenagers, one mergirl and two merboys. Skin was visible from their heads to their waists, but breathtaking muscular marine tails, shaped remarkably like legs that somehow joined in the middle, were in place where legs would be expected. Colorful scales caught the sunlight and covered the bottom half of the beings, down to a tapered point where magnificent fins the size of mature palm fronds sprouted.

Although their skin was tan, each was a slightly

different hue that seemed to match its tail. One merboy had a bright green tail with subtle black accents and a large rounded fin that resembled an upside-down paisley heart. His skin was medium brown with a slight green complexion and he had dark hair. The other boy, with a fiery crimson tail, whose fins were longer and pointed at the bottom, had a much redder tone to his features. The mergirl had a regal violet tail, with fins that fanned like a fighting fish, draping long, beautiful strands of different shades all over the rocks and sand she sat upon. Her skin tone and hair had hints of violet too. Besides the tails, they didn't look so different from human teenagers on a summer day.

"Look, it's not so steep over there. We can walk down no problem, but we should move slowly, if you want to find a way to try and talk to them without frightening them," Braelok said.

"Yeah, I know. Don't forget who is in charge here," Knya admonished with a swing of her head. Braelok smiled and bowed with his hands aimed at the beach, letting her pass him. Madden and Torque giggled.

Quietly and slowly, they started toward the merpeople, hoping not to lose the opportunity. Madden was excited and nervous. He couldn't wait to see them up close, and he would certainly get his chance, although the events didn't turn out exactly as he thought they might.

They had only taken a few steps when the shadow stretched into view, floating on the breeze at the far end of the shore.

"What is that?" Madden asked.

"I don't know, but I don't think it's good," Knya

79

replied.

The shadow grew as it began to take shape, but its color never changed. As it slowly became more opaque, they recognized its form. With four cloven hooves, powerful quarters, and a spear reaching from its forehead, the thing stepped forward and stopped Madden in his tracks. It was another grisly unicorn covered in darkness. It too bore gaping wounds and chains, but this one wore a headdress of jagged metal—and it wasn't alone. A small figure sat on the unbridled beast's back, holding clumps of its hair. It was a little girl—a young-looking pale little girl with long white hair and vacant sable eyes—perched just behind the wraith's withers. She looked zombified, wrapped in dingy rags that swirled and floated around her in the wind.

"It's her. His demon girl. We have to hurry!" Knya shouted.

They raced down to the beach as the two sinister entities stepped close to the tide. The ghastly unicorn lowered the tip of its horn to the rolling waves as clouds filled the sky and covered the light of the sun. Lightning struck and thunder boomed. The young merpeople quickly began pulling themselves toward the water, but the instant the dark unicorn's horn touched the sea, the waves froze exactly as they were. The merboys and mergirl were trapped. Madden, Braelok, Knya and Torque raced to their aid.

"Stay behind us," Knya said to the young merpeople. "We can help you."

Torque hissed and then added something that sounded like the same marine language the merpeople had used earlier. He was communicating with them. The young merpeople all kept their distance but didn't stir. Braelok ran past the finned water dwellers toward the dark figures with his gleaming sword in hand.

The grim girl lifted herself to stand on the back of her phantom steed and raised her left hand high, fingers outstretched. A murk streamed forward as a whirling wind manifested in front of her and grains of sand lifted into the air, swirling. More and more, faster and faster, the grains floated and soared into the wind as it intensified. Braelok continued on a path straight for the ghouls as several small creatures leaped out of the disturbed beach, swarming straight for him and the others.

"Sea scarabs! She's possessed them! They could kill us all!" Knya yelled as she dragged her finger in the sand, making a large circle around her and the merpeople. She dropped to her knees and again started etching symbols into the grains within the circle.

Braelok swung his sword with precision and sliced through the beetles one by one. Torque leapt into the air and flew toward the deadly storm of sand and insects. Swooping in and out of the swarm, he breathed the hottest flames he could, dropping charred beetle bodies all over the beach. But there were still many aloft. The frightened merpeople huddled closer together while Madden and Knya stood between them and the danger.

"Madden, try!" Knya screamed.

There was no time to think. What could he do? He had the power, but what kind of magick should he try to call forth? Protect them, he thought, but how? He lifted his head and closed his eyes. He imagined a barrier of magick surrounding all of them, obstructing any harm and shielding them from the oncoming threat. He concentrated on his desire, and his horn began to shimmer. A few moments later, a single slim beam of sunlight sliced down through the thick, dark clouds and met with his alicorn.

The swarm of flesh-eating scarabs was presently only a few feet away from them and advancing fast. He pushed harder as his horn reflected the sunlight and sparked brighter, becoming an intense, colorful illumination.

Just as the scarabs poised to attack, the swarm split, flew around them and continued down the beach. Thousands of poisonous beetles soared by and retreated, buoyed away by the radiant display. Madden stayed planted, his horn spewing the colorful sparks until the beetles had all passed. When they were out of sight, Torque flew to Knya's side. "I'm too old for this," he said, winded.

With the scarabs out of the way, Braelok again raced toward the ghoulish pair. The rest of them all stared down the beach to see the steed with the girl on its back rear and turn, slowly fading into a dark shadow to float away on the wind as it had arrived. The evil was gone. Braelok stood his ground in anticipation for a few moments longer, but when there was no sign of any peril, he quickly rejoined his team.

"Madden, that was incredible!" Knya said. "I... I couldn't think of the right spell fast enough."

"Yeah, way to go, chap," Torque added.

"Is everyone okay?" Madden asked, looking over the unusual group.

"Yes... but not for long," the unfamiliar, strained voice of the crimson-tailed merboy answered. He spoke with an

accent that was distinct from any Madden knew. "I am Durem, and this is Larec and Aqari. We thank you for your help. But if we don't get back into the sea very soon, we may as well have been taken by the scarabs."

Knya sighed, looking over the solid waves. "The magick is thick, but I think I may be able to at least crack it a bit," she said. She etched a bit more and called for the skies to clear and the sun to shine.

"Who... or what were these creatures?" Aqari asked.

"They came when you came," Larec added.

After a pause, Torque answered. "They may have pursued us here. These creatures are a part of the reason we have come to this beach. We have traveled from Eloria bearing news and seeking counsel, among other things." Torque smiled a dragosaur smile.

"Yes, we need your help too," Knya said to the merpeople as she continued to work her magick. "Those dark creatures only have a small role in what is happening to our world. You must tell your people that there is a great evil threatening the earth once again. Surely your mages must have felt it by now."

She stepped over the edge of the frozen waves, making a fist with one hand and gripping her wrist with the other. When her fist started to glow, she opened her hand and placed her lambent palm flat on the surface of the ice. Her hand sank through, and a large crack formed that was wide enough for the young merpeople to fit through to the sea below.

Knya spoke quickly to the three water dwellers. "You may have to swim swiftly through the freezing water, but the ᵛice has not gone too deep. Please listen—you hold a great piece to this puzzle that we must solve in order to stop the evil you just witnessed. The Oracle, Omnicus, has sent us here to find it once again. We must retrieve the key of the Cosmite. The weapon must be reached in order to defend every creature in this world from a terrible danger: the sorcerer Danuk and his dark unicorns. With them cursed, he's opening a door to the outer realms that would destroy the earth." She pointed to Madden. "This is a human boy who has taken the form of a unicorn, as the oracles have foretold, and Danuk means to have him to perform the malevolent ritual. But the evil plan may be carried out with others he means to collect. Please, you must help us," she said.

Durem, the crimson-tailed merboy, looked over the strange unfamiliar quartet and paused at Madden. He stared in silence for a moment before he and his companions slowly pulled themselves from the beach, over the ice and slipped into the water.

Before fully submerging, Durem called out to them.

"I will do what I can," he said. "My people forbid any to meet with humans, but I will tell of what happened on the beach today, and I will bring them here—if I can convince them." Then he sank into the water.

There wasn't much that any of them could do but wait and see if the merpeople would return. They made camp with the shore in sight. Braelok collected some wood and Torque lit a fire as they sat under a large, pale moon that glistened over the waves. Knya enlisted Madden to help her cast the strongest cloaking wards and barrier magick she knew of to surround them.

"Do you think they'll come back?" she asked openly.

"I do," Madden answered. "The way that merboy looked at me. What he said. I felt something. We have to give them some time."

"I think they were being truthful, however young they may be. But it will ultimately be up to the elders of their people to decide whether they will help. It would serve them better to realize what's happening sooner than later," Torque said.

"They'll be back. I just hope it's before anything else comes back," Braelok said as he stirred the fire. "So that's what your big business is, eh? Pretty big indeed, I'd say—to save the world from an evil sorcerer and the darkness he wants to bring. Seems like you could use a little help, after all. And you?" he looked to Madden. "You're really a human boy? This is a taller tale than I could have made up."

"Well, if you're scared, you can always hit the road," Knya responded.

"I'm not scared, and I don't want to leave," he said.

They all ate frugally and readied themselves for sleep in their new surroundings.

"So, Braelok, favor us with more about your travels and where you come from," Torque said.

Braelok took a bite of a pear. "Well, it's been a while since anyone asked. I... grew up on a small farm, not too far from Cairo in Egypt. It was just my mom, my sister and me. My dad was French but he died when I was really young. Mom said it was some military accident. I worked that farm with my mother and my sister, and we did okay. There was a small town real close. I had some friends. It was simple and nice.

But things changed a couple years ago." He grabbed a stick and stirred the fire up again.

"What happened?" Madden asked.

Braelok was quiet for a few seconds, but he saw that they were genuinely curious about him.

"I don't like to dwell on the past, really. We all have had bad stuff happen to us, right? Well... the town got invaded, and eventually my farm did too. They were like pirates in trucks and jeeps, just taking everything. They took my mom and sister... and then they took me. We were all together for a few days, and then they separated my sister and me from my mother. It was the last time I saw her." Braelok paused again.

"And not so long ago, I escaped from one of their boats and washed up here. Been on my own ever since, figuring out a way to find them again. I have to free my mother... and make those men pay for what they did. Not sure if you wanted that story, but it's mine."

"Braelok... I'm so sorry," Madden said.

"What happened to your sister?" Knya asked.

Braelok considered the question. "She may be beyond saving," he finally said softly, and they decided not to push for anything more. Knya looked at Braelok with empathy and Torque nudged her, nodding toward Braelok. She knew he meant for her to show some form of comfort. Knya rolled her eyes but finally put her arm around Braelok. Madden wished he could do the same.

"Well, we are all certainly grateful for your way with a sword," Torque said, "and that one in particular seems to be very unique."

"I guess it's mine now. I found it on the other side of the island the day after I found myself there. I suppose it won't sound too crazy to anyone here, but it was... growing out of a tree," Braelok said. The others gave puzzled looks.

"It wasn't stuck into the tree, it was sprouting from it. A husk and petals were unfolding from it, like a blooming flower, and the sword's hilt was in the center. It was so strange. I debated on whether I should take it or not, but it was like it was presenting itself to me. So I grabbed it and it slid out without any trouble, as easily as pulling it from butter. While I held it, the blade started to shine with this sort of prismed light. It was warm and I needed a weapon, so I kept it. It's definitely not your run-of-the-mill. Check it out."

He pulled it from the scabbard he had fashioned and held it out for them to see. Its make was clean and precise. It was about two-and-a-half-feet long from the tip of its silver blade to the bottom of its silver-and-gold hilt, with cross guards embellished in detailed lines, flora and waves curving toward a short ricasso. Above the ricasso the blade widened slightly, forming pointed edges on each side, before straightening to the length of its tip. Cast into the detailing of the hilt were four gems. A small green gem adorned one end of the cross guard, and a red one the other. A yellow gem of similar size was set at the bottom of the hilt. The largest of the four was blue, triple the size of the others and set in the middle, just above the grip. There were also a few simple shapes and squiggles etched at the base of the blade. Torque thought it might be a sigil but didn't recognize it specifically. It could have just been the craftsman's design.

"Hmm, that is something," Torque said as he looked it over. "I don't know of any metal that can cut through alicorn, the substance that composes the horn of a unicorn. Maybe if the blade were made of diamond. Or, it is possible the alicorn was damaged by the curse, but improbable. The one who placed the curse would desire their power to be unhindered. Anyway, this certainly isn't an ordinary weapon, but it seems to be serving you well. Keep it as long as it does so."

Braelok nodded and slid it back into the scabbard.

"Yeah, you definitely have a cool ninja-knight thing going on," Madden said. They all giggled.

"What about you, Knya? What was it like growing up in a magickal culture? When did you start learning?" Madden asked. The fire glistened in all of their eyes as they spoke.

"Well, I've been able to make things happen for as long as I can remember. My mother used to say I was born with the energy around me. The people of my tribe usually start trying to teach children things like water working when they are around seven or eight. It has a very practical use in a village. Most can't figure it out, but I got the hang of it pretty quick.

"When my mother told the elders about my abilities and they saw for themselves, they began my training immediately. I was with the other children for part of the day, but then I was tutored along with only one other older student who was also a gifted conjurer. He decided to leave the island a couple years ago, but we were both trained to be protectors for our people—a duty I am now fulfilling.

"I didn't want it when I was younger. I remember getting so upset one time that I ran away. In my spite, I somehow managed to get to this small town somewhere on the mainland. It had rained and I was eleven years old, barefoot. I walked into a shop where I smelled something delicious. I was tracking mud all over. The chef made a big scene, called me terrible names because of the color of my skin and the way I looked. None of the other adults there said anything. They just stared at me. I had never experienced anything like that. I had watched some television and had plenty of lessons about the world up to that point. I knew what he was saying. I'm still not sure if I feel bad about making everything he touched for the next year taste like rotten cheese, but I was young and still learning.

"Anyway, it shook me up, and as I walked out of the town, I remember feeling aware of the way people were looking at me. Sort of side-eyed. I didn't want anyone to treat me like that ever again. Ever. My sage found me and brought me home, and I decided to become the perfect student," she said as she stared at the flames.

"Ignorant fools. It's unfortunate the way we have to learn about the ugliness that humans are capable of. You are an outstanding, beautiful young lady. Don't forget it," Torque squawked. Knya smiled.

"I can remember some strange things happening when I was younger. Unexplainable things. A toy moving on its own, or... almost anytime I wished for rain," Madden said. "But, I mean, I live in Florida. And sometimes these things would happen years apart. I never thought I could really have anything to do with causing any of it."

"You had magick around you even then," Knya said.

"What is it like where you're from, Madden?" Braelok asked. Madden looked at Braelok and, for some reason, was happy that he was the one to enquire.

"It's... nice, most of the time. I live in a small city. I have a good family, my mom, a brother and a sister... I only see my dad during the summers, but he's always checking in. School is usually no fun. It's not that I don't like learning new things. It's just... there are these awful boys..." He looked at Knya and she nodded.

"They're not exactly helpful to the learning environment. I really don't ever do anything to get their attention. It's the opposite. I try to avoid them and make it around school without being seen because of them. I don't even tell anyone anymore. None of the teachers do anything about it anyway, really. I don't want my mom or dad to worry, so I hide the bruises and don't tell them when things happen. My brother looks out for me when he's around, but he's in high school, and he gives me bruises of his own when he feels like it. Never again. I can't go back. I guess I couldn't anyway, like this."

Braelok stood and placed his hand behind Madden's head.

"I would make all of them bow at your feet if I had the chance," he said.

"You're safe with us," Knya added.

"Human adolescents can be vicious sometimes, the beasts," Torque offered.

"And what about you, O ancient and wise Torque?" Knya said with a giggle. "Please tell us about your many great adventures."

Torque opened his wings and stretched.

"Ha-ha," he said. "I *have* lived many lives by your standards, and I am still far from the oldest of my kind. That

91

would be a very long story... so I'll give you a few tidbits. I have called Eloria home for decades now, although I have traveled the globe over many times and lived in many places. I've often been a companion of magicians, offering guidance where I can, and I only know of a handful of other dragosaurs left in the world today. I too have felt the lash of slavery from a few kings and knights, but it has been long since those days. I've tried to offer my services to the good fight for many, many years now, which has brought me here with all of you," he said.

"We're fortunate to have your guidance," Knya said with a smile.

They talked until the fire was only embers and fell asleep, taking turns on the watch. Each one on duty couldn't shake the feeling of an ominous presence looming around them, but they made it through the night undisturbed.

Dawn arrived and the last bit of ice was carried away, disappearing into the foamy sea. The beach lay littered with beetles, fish and other marine carcasses left from the circumstances of the previous day. The two humans, the dragosaur and the unicorn boy woke and ate lightly, still unsure of when or if the message they waited for would arrive.

The morning came and went. Then noon and afternoon did the same. The sun was soon sloping toward the horizon, and the company was losing hope that the merpeople would return.

As the sun hung halfway on its decline toward the line of the sea, something stirred in the now-gentle waves. Five figures swam to the shallows this time. The young merpeople had brought two adult mermen back with them. One of the mermen was significantly older than the other. He was in good shape, but a bit wrinkled, with grey-and-white hair flowing from his head and face. The other adult appeared like a human in his thirties, with dark features. Both had a slight crimson hue to their skin.

Braelok, Madden and Knya, with Torque on her back, all stepped toward the surf and gave a respectful bow.

The aquarians all stared at Madden. The two mermen looked back at each other and nodded. Durem swam forward and spoke.

"I told my father and grandfather everything. How you helped us. What I saw," he said.

"The Oracle has sent us from Eloria to retrieve the key of the Cosmite," Torque said.

The mermen's faces became suspicious at the request. They stared hard at the band before them. After a few moments, the elder merman spoke.

"I am Zard, and this is Zarem, my son. The son of my son has told me what you did for him and his friends. We are more than grateful, but can a day be upon us when such drastic measures are called for?" he asked.

"Yes. Have you not seen dark things lurking? Look around you at this devastation. Have you not felt that something is wrong? This is not just about scarabs and dead fish," Torque responded. He then added a few vocalizations that sounded marine-like. He was speaking to them in their language again.

Zarem responded in the marine language and then spoke human words once more. "The world of men has always been dark. Why should we think this is any greater threat?"

93

"Did you not hear what your son told you? Those evil things do his bidding—Danuk, the sorcerer," Knya said.

"He's using the unicorns, turning them evil. He's collecting them so he can open a passage to the edges of our universe and let the darkness in freely. We have to stop him before he destroys the earth with you and everyone else on it," Torque said.

"Please, Father, Grandfather. This whole beach was solid yesterday, and we could have died if not for them."

The mermen looked around at the dead scarabs and carcasses of fish and sea life left from the freeze. Then they looked at the young merboys and mergirl.

After a moment, Zarem turned to address the land dwellers again. "The Council of Neptus would almost certainly condemn any communication with humans. So we must be discreet," he said as he swam forward. He seemed to have control over the water as it began to elevate him.

"We will take you to the Guardian, but it is he who will decide if you are... worthy. Which means you're going to have to come with us to meet him. And he lives very deep."

"Come with you?" Madden said. He looked to Knya, who closed her eyes and took a deep breath.

"Omnicus told me it might come to this. I'll go," she said.

"What? Knya, how?" Madden asked.

Knya reached into her satchel and retrieved a mixture of green flakes that the Oracle had given her. "With these," she said. "These herbs give the ability to survive at the lowest depths and allow lungs to get oxygen from the water."

"I'm going with you," Braelok said.

"Braelok, you have been very kind and brave on our behalf, and maybe I've... been a little harsh at times. But now that you've heard the task at hand, I need you and Torque to stay here and protect Madden."

"And what about you?" Braelok said.

"I'll be just fine," she said, reaching for a smile that wasn't quite convincing.

"I will stay with the unicorn and the dragosaur," Zard offered. "Those creatures will feel the power of the ocean if they choose to return."

"You are most gracious, Zard," Torque said.

Madden looked to Knya and knew that he could not go with her. Then, staring down at his legs and stomping hard, he let out a sullen sigh.

"We can't make a broth or swallow the herbs whole. It won't work that way," Knya said, taking off her cape.

"So how does it work?" Braelok asked.

"We have to... burn them and inhale the smoke," she replied. Madden snickered but tried to keep it quiet. Braelok and Knya giggled too.

"How long will it last?" Braelok continued as he tossed his bag to the ground and took off his shirt.

"Six, maybe eight hours. Everyone is a little different. But once it starts to work, we have to get to the water quick. We won't be able to breathe out of the water until it wears off... it's sort of serious."

"Madden, don't worry. Torque will protect you," Knya said with a smile. "And I trust them." She whispered the last part and nodded toward the merpeople.

"Madden, pay her no mind. And not to worry—we will be quite fine for the hopefully short duration, and I've got a few tricks under my wings if need be," Torque responded.

"If we're gonna do this, we better make it quick," Braelok said, stepping into the water.

Knya and Madden caught themselves and each other staring at Braelok's taut body. They both smiled and turned away. But just before they did, Madden couldn't help but notice some scars—a few pebble-sized circles on the right side of Braelok's torso and an inch long scar at the base of his neck.

"How do we know it will last long enough for us to get there and back?" Braelok asked.

"If it will last as long as you say, you will be able to reach the Guardian and return to the surface," Zard answered.

Knya reached into her satchel again, this time retrieving a very small wooden carving that looked like a flute but was bent ninety degrees at one end. "I took this peace pipe from my village. We can use it for the herbs," she said. Then she grabbed a small pinch of the mixture and placed it at the curved end of the pipe. "Hold this a second."

She handed the instrument to Braelok, then picked up a thin piece of driftwood that lay on the beach and held it out in her hand. With her other hand, she reached for the small purple pendant that hung around her neck. She held the pendant in the air and caught the sun's rays just right, aiming them at the tip of the wood. She gave it a hard look, and after a few moments, the wood began to smoke and then to burn. "Okay," she said, reaching for the pipe. Braelok handed it over.

Knya brought the burning end of the wood to where she had placed the herbs. She looked at all of them staring intently back at her.

"Well, here goes." She took a deep breath of air and exhaled. Then she placed the straight end of the pipe to her mouth and invited the smoke into her lungs. She quickly passed it to Braelok, and he did the same. They repeated this once more, and then both coughed hard.

"We have to get into the water!" Knya growled. She and Braelok stumbled into the sea and dove into the tide.

7

Into the Deep

Knya opened her eyes under the rolling waves and looked at Braelok. Neither of them wanted to take the first gulp of water into their lungs, but time was running out. They could no longer breathe above the water, and their bodies still craved oxygen for survival. After a few more long moments, with fearful faces, they each took a deep breath of the tepid water.

The merpeople had a sort of transport chariot waiting for them. They motioned them over to a large half shell that was harnessed to three marlins. Knya and Braelok got into the shell and held on tight. In an instant, they were soaring through the salt water as they followed the merpeople's flowing fins farther and farther beneath the surface of the sea.

Knya looked back to see the shoreline fade in the distance. As she looked ahead, bright purple, blue, and orange corals sprung from the rocky banks and trailed down as far as she could see. Small creatures of all shapes and color were darting this way and that in an attempt to avoid the swift escort. The sight of the foreign world below filled Knya and

Braelok with wonder as they made an effort to take it all in.

When they had traveled what seemed like a few miles, all four merpeople stopped. Ahead of them, the sea bottom vanished. Below was a vast span of blue emptiness. Zarem swam to Braelok and Knya's chariot as it halted and reached into a compartment at the front, retrieving a small glass vial. He shook it, and a dim glow shimmered from small shrimp swimming within. He then offered it to Braelok and Knya. Braelok took the gift and bowed slightly. The merman then pointed downward. Knya felt a tiny shiver of fear fighting to emerge through her determination. She looked to Braelok—confident, stoic Braelok—and was reassured… but not by much.

They paused for another bracing moment and then the merpeople dove. Knya and Braelok's chariot followed quickly after them. As they swam deeper, the sunlight, which already seemed a distant fading star, was now a universe away. Still they continued toward their judgment by an unknown entity in an unfamiliar world. Beyond them in the distance, they saw faint lights that flickered and faded. More and more began to appear and disappear as they descended.

Knya and Braelok felt as though they were deep in outer space and stars surrounded them everywhere. They lit up beautifully in every hue, some in clusters and formations like swirling galaxies that gave the divers charmed excitement as they were carried through the depths. But after what seemed like several more miles drifting through a fathomless abyss, the awe began to wear off: They soon felt lost and worries of betrayal began to take shape in their minds.

Perhaps the mermen had been against them from the

beginning. Perhaps they were simply trying to play some terrible game of torture before killing them. Torque and Madden were alone up there, and what did they all really know about these water creatures anyway? Had they made a mistake to trust them so quickly? And how long had they been down here? The magick of the herbs might be half used up by now. Knya used the sun to tell time, but the light of the sun was completely lost in the deep. She shared a pensive look with Braelok. They knew the same questions were in each of their thoughts. Their feelings began to escalate into anxiety, when something firm manifested below. They had reached the bottom.

The chariot shell came to a halt and settled on the ocean floor. Knya and Braelok scanned their surroundings but could barely make out anything. It was just so dark, even with the glowing shrimp. Knya then placed her purple gem in her hand and held it above her head. She closed her eyes for just a moment and the rock erupted with light. She smiled at Braelok.

The merpeople all looked a bit surprised. The land dwellers could now glimpse the vastness of their environment. A rocky ocean floor went as far as they could see, flecked with a few odd-looking fish and crustaceans. Zarem swam ahead a few feet with something cupped in his hands. He raised it to his lips, and Knya realized it was some sort of carved twisted shell. As he forced water through it, a beautiful sound emerged. He repeated this once more and then was still. For a few moments, all of them remained in place and waited. For what, Knya and Braelok had no idea, but they stayed alert.

Then, suddenly, the ocean floor beneath them erupted and quaked. What had been sure footing only moments before now began to rise and cast a cloud of sediment so intense they were all once again blinded. Knya barely heard her own scream in the enormity of the commotion. Fear pulsed through her body and she reached for Braelok, finding his hand as he reached for hers.

He and Knya swam for their lives through the cloudy water as the ground continued to shift below them. They both realized they had been resting on something that was alive—and it was something humongous. With Knya's stone still shining, they slowed for a moment, hoping to gain some bearings. As the sediment settled, they peered in every direction, searching for the merpeople, trying to view any sign of life through the haze.

What they finally saw was a sight of terror. A gigantic sea creature bigger than anything either of them had ever seen was only yards away. It was larger than a blue whale, yet it had a striking bony deep sea anatomy, with a wide head and starkly spined dorsal and pectoral fins splaying from its ridged long body, which eventually tapered to a frayed length of a tailfin—and it was coming straight for them. All either of them could think was that the mermen had lied. They had delivered them into a trap and given them to a fearsome beast. Or perhaps they weren't worthy of the Guardian after all, and this leviathan had come to devour them. It didn't move with haste, and yet it was so huge that its simple motions were great. It opened its mouth to bare huge, serrated barb-tipped teeth as it continued to advance.

The two air-breathing humans, who were now at the bottom of the ocean, turned and swam as fast as they could. Their attempt was nearly futile. The giant animal was upon them. They looked back to see the razor teeth passing over their heads and then advancing in front of them. They were in the creature's mouth. Knya let out another ocean-muted scream as she realized what was happening. They swam with all their might, trying to fight past the boundary of the incredible mandibles. But they only fell further into its vastness. Escape was impossible. One chomp and their fate was sealed.

But just when all hope seemed lost, the animal stopped. Its mouth never closed and it settled back to the ocean floor. Knya and Braelok kept swimming, and as they neared their exit, something caught Braelok's eye. Below them, the animal had pulled back its tongue, and a small shining object reflected Knya's light.

They swam out of the beast's mouth, past the huge deadly points, and saw that the merpeople were waiting for them. The merpeople were stoic in their disposition and simply pointed back at the sea giant that lay in front of them with jaws open. Braelok thought about what he had seen in its mouth. Perhaps all was not what it seemed. He looked at Knya, and they both nodded.

They swam to the edge of the jagged mandibles, and she cast her light in where he pointed. There, far below in the creature's mouth, something glistened. They shared a final look, and Braelok dove as fast as he could in the direction of the glimmering object, deep into the gargantuan beast's maw. He approached the glinting thing and realized it was a key, very tiny in size—especially tiny to be inside such a large creature's mouth. They had found it. An important piece of the puzzle was finally in place.

Braelok retrieved the key and again swam past the sharp teeth of the beast that he now knew was an ally—

a peculiar, ancient friend and trusted protector of this important relic. As Braelok gripped the small key, he looked back at the colossal creature. He stared deep into its huge eyes and felt a connection, and a sense of encouragement that he was a part of something incredible. He then turned to Knya, and they swam back to the large shell where the merpeople were waiting.

The group wasted no time, and as quickly as they had descended, they started for the surface. Knya and Braelok took in the last sights of this beautiful, alien world as they made their way upward, back in the direction they had come. When they reached the reef again, they looked at each other for a moment and smiled, feeling joy at their contribution and accomplishment. But a moment was all they were permitted.

Knya's smile left her almost immediately. She grabbed her throat and then her chest. A look of panic filled her eyes as she attempted to swim. Braelok knew what was happening. It was wearing off. The herbs that had granted them asylum in the water for a limited period were no longer in effect, and Knya was drowning. Braelok pulled her back to the swiftly moving shell, knowing she could swim no faster. The look on her face was terrifying even to Braelok as he tried to do all he could. The merpeople understood what was taking place and increased their haste.

In the distance ahead, the boundary of the sea slowly became visible. The surface was near, and a last sliver of crimson sunlight still glistened on the waves above. *Almost there*, Braelok thought, *just a little longer*. But before they broke the surface of the water, the life left Knya's body. She lay motionless as they pulled her limp frame onto the shore.

"Knya!" Madden cried as he and Torque raced to them. Braelok choked and vomited as he tried to tend to Knya. His body had not yet readjusted to the surface.

"She ran out of time, but it is not too late," Zarem said as he pulled himself beside her and placed his hands on her chest. Zard quickly pulled himself to her opposite side. He placed his hand on her forehead and closed his eyes, then made a symbol above her brow with his finger.

"Get me some leaves or fruit from the trees. Quickly! But it must be from the trees, it must be alive," he said. Torque did so and returned with both, dropping them into Zard's hands. Zard held them over Knya's head and mumbled some unintelligible sounds. As he did, the fruits and leaves in his hands began to change from green and healthy to wilted brown.

Once Braelok's breathing returned to normal, he moved quickly to Knya's side with the rest of the frightened company. Madden lowered his head, bringing his horn close to her, and it began to flicker. He knew he had power, although he still wasn't exactly sure how to control it. He thought of how the Oracle, Torque, Braelok, the merpeople and this beautiful girl who was now somewhere between life and death had all come together in an attempt to save the Earth, to save and protect the entire world as they knew it. With such a task, they all knew danger was inherent, but they couldn't lose her now.

The next moments passed like hours as they waited for a sign of breath. Still limp and motionless, Knya lay on the now dusk-drenched sandy beach surrounded by her companions.

And then a cough erupted and a gasp followed. Liquid splashed out of her mouth and she began breathing.

They all let out sighs and cheers of relief. Both mermen quickly returned to the waves as the breath returned to Knya's body. Braelok, Torque and Madden all tended to her as they called out thanks to their water-dwelling allies. Just before disappearing into the surf, Zard spoke one last time.

"We will share your story. The merpeople will know of Danuk and this evil. Your retrieval of the key and the unicorn child before us is an omen, and we wish you the strength of the ocean when you face this adversary of us all. Perhaps there is hope for the future of our people," he said. With that, all five merpeople turned and leaped into the rolling waves.

Braelok slowly opened the clutch of his grasp to look at what he had retrieved from the depths. In the center of his sand-covered palm was a tiny brass key. It was around two inches long and looked like it was made for a child's doll. But it was also intricate and antique. He wondered what it was for. *What did it open? And how was it going to be used against the darkness?*

8

Stolen

A young dark-haired boy with tan skin and russet-umber gemstone eyes slammed a long stick with a sharp piece of lead wedged in the top downward through rocky soil. The sun was high and the field vast. Row after row, he overturned the earth to sow his crops. The sound of horses calling to each other rang out on the wind and carried far as the echoes soared down the hills through the fertile green valley. Ahead of the boy to the east was a small wooden cottage with a large hole on one side of the roof that was poorly patched. A woman and a young girl holding hands on the porch called out to him in the field. Their voices were calm as they smiled and waved. The boy's eyes widened and lit up. His lips revealed a happy wholesome smile as he returned the wave with enthusiasm.

"I'm so proud of you, Braelok. You make your mother proud," the woman said as she and the girl continued to wave with delight.

Then, a moment after she spoke, a strange buzzing crept over the hills, slowly intensifying, replacing the whinnying of horses. The boy examined the land around him curiously, and something edged into his view from the west. At first, just a few dots in the distance, but as more and more seemed to rise out of the horizon, he realized what the sound was. It was the coughing grinding growls of crudely repaired gas engines, and then something else rang out. From the vehicles, gunfire sprayed, laying waste to livestock as they passed. It was presently clear that what had arrived was dangerous, deadly.

The smiles and waves of joy were quickly replaced with shrieks of panic and terror as the woman screamed for her children. The boy raced straight toward the cottage and held fast to his tool, knowing that although he was not yet a man, he would have to defend his family.

Faster and harder, the boy ran, calling out to his mother, but the cottage was still far. Tears swelled in his russet-umber eyes and ran down his cheeks as the twisted human predators advanced closer. His mother cried out for him again, clenching his baby sister tight against her frantic body. The field seemed to expand, and against his greatest will, he could not reach the home where his family screamed in terror. His legs weak but still giving everything, he called out to them once more.

As he exhaled the desperate cry, he saw the dirty, barbarous thugs approach the house where he had grown up with his mother and sister. They rushed the porch and seized the woman and child, ignoring their horrified screaming.

The screaming.

Those screams would stay with the boy for life, unwelcomed, becoming audible from time to time, as he could never forget. Then everything that surrounded him fell away, and a face that wasn't quite human loomed over him, sneering. It was the last thing Braelok saw before he was jolted from his sleep. He leaped from his bed in a cold sweat.

He scanned his surroundings. As he slowly remembered where he was, he composed himself. They had camped on the beach once more after the fright and excitement of the day's events. The night was brisk, and the embers of the fire were still aglow, so he stirred them back to a flame and warmed himself.

"Can't sleep?" Madden's voice was soft as he lifted his head.

"You could say that. Just a bad dream. One that visits on occasion," Braelok said.

"What happens in the dream?" Madden asked.

"Just shadows from the past," Braelok replied.

"Sleep has been a little strange for me lately too. My dreams get... crossed. I often start out as a unicorn, but then it's always revealed somehow that I'm just a boy. I feel the disappointment. I get really upset, and then I wake up and I'm back in this body. I know all of this is new. I guess I'll get used to it. A few days ago I wouldn't have believed any of this." Madden watched the fire as he spoke.

"So, how are you holding up? Seems like a lot of responsibility, from what I understand," Braelok said.

Madden made a small gesture resembling a shrug. "Sometimes I think this *is* all just a dream. When I saw the unicorn for the first time, in front of my eyes... I had never witnessed that kind of magick before. I've read books and heard stories and made up my own stories, but they were just that. Stories. Fiction. Then it happened. I'm not even exactly sure how. And honestly... I'm scared about the future now that I know what's at stake. I know what everyone has been telling me, and I sort of know what we're supposed to do, but what if... what if something else goes wrong? What if we make some other mistake?"

"I think all we can do is to do our best." Braelok nodded toward Knya. "She was brave enough to risk her life, and maybe that's what we all have to do. I've had to fight for my life plenty already, and I'm not going to let anyone destroy the good things that we still have. We won't fail. We have to do everything we can to stop... whatever his name is before it's too late. With this weapon, it sounds like it's possible, and now we're all in this together. And really, anyone that wants to survive is in this with us, even if they don't know it." He gave Madden a hopeful smile and patted his head. Madden returned the smile as best he could.

"I'm really happy you're with us, Braelok. We might not have made it without you."

9

Magick

The journey back was uneventful and hurried. Back the way they came, through the forest toward the east, they traveled to Eloria to share with Omnicus what they had encountered and achieved. They camped in a small meadow along the way and began again the following day. Knya rested on Madden's back while she regained her strength. She finally stirred from a nap as the sun was mid-sky.

"How are you?" Madden asked his cargo.

"I've felt better... but a definite improvement," Knya said.

"You sure scared us."

"I'm just keeping you on your toes... or hooves," she joked as she pulled her cape tighter.

"You two ought to be very proud of yourselves. It was very brave what you did," Torque said, poking his head out of Knya's satchel.

"I wish you both could have seen everything down there. It was incredible," Braelok said.

"I felt your magick, Madden," Knya said. "When I was

still underwater and I couldn't breathe anymore, there was a point where I felt like I had left my body. I think I might have been more than just unconscious. There was this sort of... gentle feeling, pulling me one way. I couldn't stop. I didn't want to. But then I heard you calling to me and I knew I was needed. I felt a burst of energy all through me. And then I woke up."

"The mermen used some magick of their own to wake you, but I tried to help. I was calling. I tried as hard as I could to see you healthy again, awake and smiling."

"Must have helped, because I knew it was you, calling me back." As she spoke, they came to the top of a hill. On the other side, Eloria could be seen far in the distance.

"Ah, thanks be to the goodness. We've almost made it," Torque said.

The words gave Madden a sense of comfort, although he knew that they had only achieved the first part of their task, and another trial was to come.

"What is that over there?" Knya pointed above the island's mountain range. "That's not any bird I've ever seen."

Soaring high over the mountains was a huge black-and-grey creature that none of them could quite make out.

"You got me, but I think we better lay low until it passes," Braelok said. The creature continued to soar away from them, and soon it was out of sight.

They reached the fortress late in the evening and finally felt a bit of safety within its walls. Meirvot greeted them and had a meal waiting. Omnicus had requested to be awakened should they arrive, but since it was so late and all of them were exhausted, Torque insisted they all rest and share what they had learned in the morning. No one contested. They were shown to their sleeping quarters and quickly fell into slumber.

The next morning, after a much-needed night of good sleep, they went to see the Oracle. He looked exactly as he had when they had left him, draped over his throne, with fruits and food being brought to him. They stepped into the gazebo and his amber elephant face filled with relieved delight.

"Hellooo! I'm so happy you all are safe and soun—" The Oracle didn't finish his words but stared straight at Braelok and was silent for a few moments.

"Omnicus?" Torque flew over to the eccentric elephant.

"Ohh, I'm sorry, I must have dozed. Ummmhh." He cleared his throat. "Who is this strapping young stranger before me?"

"His name is Braelok," Madden offered. "He saved our lives in the forest, and he helped Knya get the key."

"I don't know if we could have done it without him," Knya added.

"Goodness me. Saved your lives? Well, Braelok, it seems you were a blessing to be in those woods. And at just the right time," Omnicus said.

Braelok was quiet for a moment. "Yes, blessings don't always come in the packages we expect," he replied with a smile.

"Hmmm, hmmm. Yes, very true."

They presented Omnicus with the brass key and told him every detail of their journey. They told him of the encounter with the demon child and the dark unicorns and of

113

the merpeople and the great sea creature. They recounted Braelok's brave actions and the extraordinary circumstances surrounding his sword, giving the amber elephant a chance to look it over thoroughly. Omnicus remarked its strong aura and stated that it was certainly uncommon. When they told him of Knya having to be revived, he was fraught with concern, ordering her to eat guava and drink peppermint tea and to inhale the vapors. He was also very interested in Madden's magickal efforts against their attackers.

"Those dark creatures... on this island? My gracious, it may already be worse than I thought. I hope my spells can continue to keep us hidden here," the Oracle said. "I'm happy to hear you're using your gifts, Madden. Hmm. Tapping into it may be difficult at first, but you must keep trying to learn and get stronger."

"Oh, I want to," Madden said. "I really want to know more about what is possible. About what I can... what we can do."

The Oracle gazed at him in his regular blank fashion, like he was seeing something other than what was in front of him, and then he spoke.

"I believe you rather should learn a few things. The state of affairs has only become more hazardous, and you should have some technical magickal instruction, regardless of whether you decide to join in the next task or not. Will you walk with me, Madden, hmm?" Omnicus asked as he stepped down from his seat, and placed his front appendages on the ground, walking on all fours. Madden looked at him and then around at the others before answering.

"Yeah, sure," he said.

He and Omnicus wandered out into the gardens and admired some sculptures before the elephant paused just in front of a statue that stood at the opposite side of the courtyard from the gazebo. Similar to the depiction of the fountain, the statue featured the figures of a human, a merfolk, a centaur and a dragon, all entangled by a large serpent beneath a rearing unicorn whose horn was surrounded by flames. Here the conversation segued to something more serious.

"How have you enjoyed being a unicorn thus far, aside from the perils you've had to behold?" Omnicus asked.

Madden weighed the question. "Well, I could have gone my whole life without ever wanting to see or be chased by one of those scary Night of the Living Dead things, but to be honest, it's been amazing," he said. "I know this must have been part of my wish, deep down. And when I did the magick, when I was responsible for making it happen, capable of making it happen, it felt more than good. It felt incredible. It felt right. Like this is exactly what I am supposed to be doing, finally. I'm not ready to be an ordinary boy again. I'm not sure if I ever will be."

"Well, it's lovely to hear that there is some merriment to accompany the uneasiness that you have had to endure, hmm hmm. And your magick will only grow." Omnicus then turned his attention to the statue and continued. "Madden, there is more information that I must impart to you and I hope you'll forgive me for having to do so. Everything I have relayed to you so far is very true and very serious, as you have unfortunately seen some of these dangers for yourself now. But I must explain further. There is even more to this wild situation, and your significance in it is even greater than what

115

you have as yet been told. I must now tell you how the Cosmite came to be and what it requires to work." Madden listened intently as the amber elephant spoke.

"Long, long ago, when the planet was a bit younger and man was a new species, darkness again came to the lands and seas. It was a terrible nightmare of a time that I would not have wanted to be around for. The wizards and sorcerers of old faced a great adversary not unlike the one we face now. In the mounting danger, the beings of the planet all fought together and were victorious after certain powerful measures were discovered and exercised.

"Much was lost, but life survived. In order to protect the future of the earth and all of the creatures here should darkness return again, a great weapon was fashioned. They poured their most potent magick into this talisman so darkness could be vanquished once more. That is how the Cosmite was created, and although powerful, it still needs a vessel in order to be used. At that time, unicorns were not so few, and because of their magickal potential, they were chosen as the tangible conduit for the weapon's power," Omnicus explained, indicating the stone form in front of them. "Worn like a crown of fire upon the horn, this will require you, Madden. You are the vessel." Madden looked at the statue in a daze.

"There have been many prophecies and many heroes on this earth and throughout the universe, some possessing extraordinary gifts, who are called upon in order to defend the greater good. I spoke of the light you have always had around you, but when you changed, when you merged with this form, you became something even greater. Something this world has never produced. Altogether, you're a marvel of magick. When you shifted, your light became magnified. That light... I have seen your light in my dreams, and it is needed to channel the power of the Cosmite.

"Once again, this is your choice, Madden. But we are unaware of anyone else that might be able to defeat Danuk. Although there may be other unicorns somewhere, we have seen none for decades. I know this is a terrible burden, and you are just beginning to understand your power, but you, little one, you are hope for my soul and for the souls of everyone, if you'll continue to be brave and take it on. I really am honored to be in your company."

Madden breathed deeply and shifted his gaze to the scenery that surrounded him. From where they stood he had a tremendous view of the island below. The scale and beauty of it all helped to calm and encourage him. He was quiet for a few seconds before answering.

"I'm scared, but if this is what I have to do to make everyone safe, I'll do it. Can you help me learn how to use magick? How it really works?" Madden asked.

"I'll do all I can in the short time we've been granted." Omnicus replied. "We can start immediately."

"Okay," Madden said. "Can I have a few minutes to myself?"

"Of course. I'll join the others, and await you there."

Omnicus turned back toward the gazebo, and Madden took a walk around the parts of the yard that he hadn't yet explored. At its edge he found a few stairs that led down to a grassy area of hedges and pear trees that provided perfect solitude. He knelt there, trying to relax and ease his mind for a few moments alone before he returned to his friends, but he was finding it troublesome to sort his thoughts. How had so much responsibility fallen upon him? He barely knew how to call upon any magick at all. How was he to be the one to channel this great weapon's power? How did it work, and what if he failed? What if they had all made a dire mistake in believing he would be of any use against this overwhelming threat? What if he fell victim to this dangerous evil, or perished because he wasn't rightly prepared?

He closed his eyes, making an effort to inhale and exhale fully, and listened to the sounds of nature around him: the wind through the leaves, a gull calling far in the distance, a grasshopper making its way through the lush soft green blades he laid upon. *What choice did he have, except to do everything he could to protect this world and the loved ones that dwelled in it?*

He knew time was pressed, so he didn't stay long. After a few more minutes of contemplation, wondering what this new requirement would bring, he pulled himself up and marched back to the pillared stone structure.

"I am now your student," he said to Omnicus and Knya.

"Most excellent, hmm, hmm." Omnicus stood upright with his front legs crossed, tapping his chin. "Hmmm, where to begin? There are all kinds of magick, Madden. Some of the simplest things hold real and true magick. Simply being kind to someone has the power to completely alter their state of being and the energy that makes up their physical matter. Likewise, being cruel or condescending can usurp or steal energy. In the first scenario, both beings benefit, their energies increasing. In the second, it may seem that acquiring energy in this way strengthens the taker but it is quickly dissipated, leaving an emptiness that must be filled again. This is magick, perhaps in a most elementary form, but it is real.

Magick is everywhere, and it is what makes everything in the universe work... or function. It is running through us now and we are all part of it. Like molecules or atoms of an unimaginably smaller scale, it makes up everything. It is this general understanding that is the basis of the details of the practical manipulation of this energy. We can cause changes to the..." Omnicus spun his front foot above the ground and tiny pebbles began to gather and lift into the air, forming into a pearl as he spoke. Madden watched, fascinated. "... conformity or organization of matter and make things happen through our will, with a few other small yet sometimes theatrical procedures." With another wave of his front foot the pearl became pebbles again and fell to the ground.

Omnicus paused as Madden gave him a puzzled look. "Hmm, hmm, I know it seems a lot, but once you can understand this, you can manipulate and wield that energy, which is the practice that is usually referred to as magick. There are many different ways to do so, but the mind is truly where our magick begins. When we strengthen our minds in the physical understanding, we can tap into the structure and architecture of the world around us to make the changes we call upon. Learning to express your will clearly is fundamental in practicing magick.

"Our words..." Omnicus enunciated as translucent glowing letters floated out of his mouth. W-O-R-D-S settled in front of him before dissipating like mist. Madden laughed. "... are the sonic manifestation of our inner thoughts and desires, and they can be powerful when used properly. Vocalization is the most basic way of making our will known and casting our intentions out into the ether of the universe. The repetition of an incantation can often strengthen it.

"But of course it's not just that simple. You still have to find a way to make your intentions have an effect on the outside world... a way to make the reality around you accept your will and recreate it accordingly. This is where the many types and methods of magick one can find, if they search hard enough, have come from--the many attempts by beings since the dawn of thought to tap into this power and use it.

"You could compare it to music, I suppose," Omnicus continued his lecture. "There are rules and framework, and you can even make up your own if you know how. But we most often refer to previously collected data of works and experiments. The library here is more than satisfactory, but there have been countless books upon the craft that have been destroyed in order to extinguish this knowledge and keep people from discovering their potential. We also know that some places and *things* carry innate magickal attributes, and that others can be empowered by a practitioner, for various purposes. Eloria is a place where magick swells."

"Or like the stone I use," Knya chimed in. "It's opalium. It naturally gives magick a little kick, but mine has a few added enhancements. It was passed down through my family."

"Like the Cosmite?" Madden said.

"Precisely," Omnicus said. "The Cosmite was created this way, empowered by many, on an incredible scale. I believe I mentioned before that there are some *beings* that are predisposed to using the power too. For some it's like an instinct, and some only master certain abilities. Fairies, florafels, perpeneo butterflies, some merpeople and many others are like this, but unicorns are among the most powerful creatures known to history. Alicorn has been sought after for millennia, yet contrary to belief, although it has strong magickal properties, it is not the source of a unicorn's power, only the point where energy is most naturally released."

Madden's eyes zipped up toward his own horn. It was set too high for him to actually see, but he took account of Omnicus's words.

"Magick is also accessible to many humans. Perhaps all humans could be taught to some extent, although most just seem simply hopeless. But I suppose the same could be said about teaching calculus or particle physics. Human magicians most often use spells that are combinations of words or signs, with different minerals or plants that help to cause certain specific changes. Some do strengthen their magick by channeling it through gems or wands, but these are not necessary for all magickal workers. A magician with an adept understanding alone can generate very large amounts of energy. You've been doing it all on your own. The power of the unicorn form you've taken has and will continue to enhance your abilities, and the more you practice the stronger you'll become."

"So why don't I see any magick when I'm home or at school or when I'm walking to the supermarket? I mean, why doesn't anyone know about all of this?" Madden questioned further.

"Well, some do, and scientists are actually discovering more and more all the time, although they have different ways of saying it. Magnetism is a simple example. We can easily see its influence, yet the force is invisible. And just because man can now see the boundaries of the earth from space doesn't mean that there are no secrets or mysteries to be discovered.

"But I do concede people are mixed up these days. They aren't sure what to believe or what the truth is. Some are afraid to look for the truth. They don't understand that our minds are a gift. The expression of our being! The house of the soul! Capable of incredible things, and this is where all of our power is truly stored.

"For some reason, many of the world's institutions have been twisted to forbid the use of the full extent of our potential. Many lives throughout history have been extinguished because they showed even the slightest hints of a magickal gift. It is an unfortunate plan to keep people devout and controlled."

Madden thought of the witch trials in Massachusetts as Omnicus continued.

"This is exactly contrary to what we should do. We should be using our magick to nurture, help, and bring the wounded to a higher love and state of existence." Omnicus went on.

"What about Danuk? Why is he able to do such terribly evil things?" Braelok had stood by quietly listening but now spoke up.

"Like every creature, there is light and dark within him too. He has chosen the darker side of the magick. He is extremely old and seems to have a very strong understanding of how to manipulate the power," Omnicus said.

"If that's true, then what does he stand to gain?" Madden asked.

"Magick he isn't capable of accomplishing himself, as is the usual catalyst for turning to the dark," Omnicus answered. "A magician, as far as we understand, can only gather and discharge so much energy, even at a master level, although this limit is of some debate in itself and may vary slightly with the individual. Our mortal bodies are only capable of so much. Danuk wants to use the unicorn's energy to release a dark spirit of even greater power to give him control over the earth. But he is blinded, foolishly deceived, and that spirit will destroy the planet and all who dwell upon it if it is not stopped," Omnicus added.

"Could our magick hurt anyone? I mean, if we needed to protect ourselves?" Madden asked. "Is magick only good or bad, or is it the one who's using it?"

"I dare not say that pain is the only way to deal with an adversary... but there are certainly spells and rituals that are benevolent, some that are malevolent, and some in the area in between. There are evil spirits and wicked intentions and scarred souls seeking revenge. But our magick, your magick, comes from inside you. You are responsible for the events you spin into motion just as you would be without using magick. And the repercussions of each will almost certainly present themselves sooner than later, although that is not always the case. So, it serves a magician best to keep their magick clean and, for the most part, simple. Do as you will, but be thoughtful of what you send out into the world, as it may come back to visit you. Anyway, let's give it a try, should we? Hmm, hmm, come on."

The amber elephant walked out of the gazebo and over to the fountain, and they all followed. He raised his arm over a spout and some water splashed forward, hovering in the air in front of him. "Water is a great substance to start learning magick with, my little unicorn. It is smooth and more easily influenced than solid matter. We'll start here and try to move through a few basics."

Each lesson began a bit cumbersome as Madden tried to apply their advice and reproduce each effect. He had really only accomplished any charms before during heightened emotional situations, and the calm practical study was considerably different. They started with simply pushing shallow puddles, and then progressed to lifting the water into the air and shaping it. Something like handgun target practice followed as several small stones were lined up and he was instructed on how to create energy blasts, which was really just an extension of the first lesson.

The next exercise was more difficult. Shifting the construction of solids took more energy and made Madden feel woozy after he finally managed to perform it. Using verbal incantations for the specific references, he changed a piece of dead wood into stone, and then, more complicatedly, turned a leaf into a feather.

They ended his full day of education with meditation and garnering his energy. As the sun slouched behind the mountains and into the ocean, Omnicus let out a yawn. "Hmm, well, I think we have done enough for today. You've done terrifically and accomplished more than I imagined you would, hmm, hmm. Dinner should be prepared soon. You all will remain here tonight so you may rest, although time is still of grave importance, and we must get you to the Cosmite. We can discuss the journey after we've had something to eat."

Madden stretched. "Thank you all, for your help

today. It was... cooler than cool. Wizard's Hall, look out," he said with a unicorn smile.

"You did great." Knya chuckled, even though she didn't quite get the reference.

"Indeed," Torque agreed. "Now let's go and see about that dinner." They all laughed.

In the dining room they were joined by Tajre and Meirvot, and Madden learned that they were both magicians, only minor ones who could never really crack the more difficult magick. They seemed to relish their positions as aides to the Oracle. Madden, Knya, Braelok and Torque all ate their fill and heard Omnicus's tales of his childhood in a laboratory and his liberation to Eloria. Yet, he still never mentioned the magickal constraints that kept him trapped within the boundaries of the castle grounds. Madden wondered what the intimate details were but certainly wasn't going to bring it up. After dinner, there was a particular sweet cake that everyone had second helpings of, and a few had thirds.

They sat around the table, full and content, nearly forgetting the dangerous mission that had called them there, until Omnicus brought the subject back to mind. "Now, a few details must be discussed. The venture that lies ahead may have its own perils. This journey is much farther than the Sound. You cannot go on foot. To keep it safe from evil, the weapon was taken among the highest peaks on earth and hidden in an enchanted box within a room of light. The key was fashioned and, for further protection, hidden at the greatest depths with those whom you've already met. The key had to be obtained in order to unlock the protection of the box that is within this room of light, and now the key must be taken there, to the ancient Power Keep amidst the peaks of the Himalayas, where the weapon should have remained."

Tajre and Meirvot cleared the table as Omnicus continued. "The temple was once a place of learning as well as safekeeping for the weapon, and magicians of all sorts were educated in their gifts, sharing knowledge with one another. The gates of the Keep were forged from the minerals of the meteors of Oryn, said to be unbreakable, and, when polished, to shine like no other metal. Magick flourished in the temple for an age, but eventually, things changed. It was a very different place last I visited, and even that was years ago.

"The Himalayas are a considerable journey, so we will have to use magick to send you. Because the Keep lies on the other side of the earth, the time of day also differs, and we will need to wait until after tomorrow's sunset here to transport you. When night has come to Eloria, we will relocate you to daylight within the mountain range of the Himalayas. I have not yet received word from the Power Keep, but there should still be a guardian that remains. Beware, yet with Madden and the key you should be permitted, and I will do all I can to continue efforts of informing the Keep of the predicament. Between the two of you, Madden and Knya, and with the further help of the guardian you shouldn't have much trouble returning to Eloria as we have sent you. We will decide our further plan of action when you have returned, and I will try my best to observe your progress from afar."

They all looked to one another, and were quiet for a moment.

"We've made it this far, and we must continue with vigilance," Torque said.

"Knya, are you well enough to continue so soon?" Omnicus asked.

"I'm fine, and after another good night's sleep, I'll be even better," she said.

"Madden?" Omnicus asked.

Madden nodded. "Yes," he said.

Omnicus smiled. "We'll continue your lessons after this measure," he said.

"I'm in too, if you'll let me," Braelok offered.

"Well, I don't see why not," Torque said.

"We could use an extra hand," Knya agreed.

Omnicus paused, thoughtfully looking at Braelok. "I think you all will benefit from the help of one another," the amber elephant said. "Alas, we do want to be sure you're all able to get a good night's sleep before you make for the mountains come tomorrow, and you can certainly sleep in through the morning."

They were all beginning to feel drowsy as the day and their meals caught up with them, and soon they retired to their separate quarters.

None of the guests of the castle stirred from their beds before noon the following day. Being able to sleep in with no appointments to wake you is a superb magick of the most divine type. Madden and Braelok emerged around the same time and headed for the dining room, hoping for some leftover breakfast. They found Omnicus sitting with Torque and his companions at the table, which was set with a few bowls of nuts, fruits and greens. The Oracle plucked at a large platter with his trunk. It seemed everyone had had a bit of a late morning. Braelok and Madden joined them.

When the boys finished eating they sat relaxed at the table. "You've got something right here," Braelok pointed to Madden's shoulder. Madden fell for it, eyeing the spot as Braelok lightly tapped his unicorn nose and snickered.

Madden shook his head smiling before laughing himself. Knya was the last to rouse and take a seat at the table with the others. They all had a few more hours of calm before they had to begin the next task of their mission, and no one seemed too anxious to get going.

After breakfast, Madden, Braelok and Knya walked through the castle. In one corridor they came to a wall with several portraits hanging. Knya explained that they were the oracles of the past. Most of them were of human-looking beings, but a few stood out. There was one of an ebony-skinned male child, one of a fair-complexioned female with an enlarged head, one of a scaly reptile-looking creature, another of a handsome, young tan male human who had wings reaching from his shoulders, one a set of female twins who were identical except for the left twin having jet hair and skin and the other being completely albino, and one of a middle-aged man who appeared of Asian descent and had four arms instead of two. Omnicus was the final portrait displayed in the sequence.

They took a stroll out into the yard past the gazebo, and Madden decided to practice some of his magickal teachings, making a few shapes in the fountain water before lifting some nearby cuts of stone into the air. He struggled as they got heavier but managed to lift a block that two strong men would have had trouble carrying. Madden was excited and relieved each time he saw his magick working, diligently trying to sharpen his skills, finding his vision occasionally wandering to eye the statue of the crowned unicorn that lay just beyond them in the yard.

Meandering around the perimeter of the grounds they explored the plentiful flora while butterflies and dragonflies drifted about, dipping into a beautiful plethora of open blooms. Toward a far corner the trio approached a willow tree, which draped a canopy of leafy branches that nearly reached the ground. Knya parted the hanging limbs and motioned them inside. "Check it out." They followed her through to find a striking bushel of flowers growing beneath the cover of the tree. "These are my favorite." She lowered her head to smell a blossom. The flowers displayed a star shaped outer ring of petals with a single inner row of thinner, delicate strands that surrounded a pollen dusted pronged stigma, all decorated in splashes of violet, magenta, blue, yellow and white. "Look closer. Notice anything?" Madden and Braelok examined the flowers and saw what she was referring to. The flowers were faintly luminous.

"Oh, wow. They're glowing," Madden said.

"Yeah, they're called burning passion flowers and they only grow here on Mythras, as far as I know," Knya explained.

"So cool." Braelok admired the blooms.

"You should see them at night to really get the full exhibition. That's when they're the brightest," Knya said. Turning to continue walking, she shifted her satchel from her shoulder and it slipped out of her hand onto the ground.

Braelok retrieved it. "My lady," he said, offering it to her in an exaggerated, chivalrous manner.

Knya rolled her eyes. "Thanks," she said. She and Braelok laughed. Madden smiled too, but felt a slight unexpected twinge in his abdomen upon hearing Braelok say those words to her, seeing Braelok's display. Madden banished the unpleasant feeling at once when he realized what it was, embarrassed for having let it exist at all. He shook it off and laughed with them, resuming his enjoyment of the beautiful foliage.

They walked down the stairs, under the pear trees along the hedges and then ate a healthy meal. They enjoyed as much of the day as they could, but soon the time to ready themselves for their journey had arrived. As the sun slid low, casting rosy, lavender tints throughout the castle, everyone met in the entrance hall. Electrical lights and candles illuminated the room. Omnicus sat on a large carved chair with his assistants nearby.

"I suppose the time has come, my dears. We must get you to the temple. Knya, I'm giving the key to you. Keep it safe," Omnicus said. The small brass shape floated from his trunk into the air. Knya reached for it and placed it on her necklace, next to her gem.

"The preparations, please," Omnicus called to Tajre and Meirvot. They brought Knya and Braelok each a sack filled with fruit, nuts and bread, and a leather pouch filled with water.

"The temple is hidden by geography and magick in a desolate area within the eastern region of the mountains, near Everest. There are other dangers on the mainland too. You must be careful to stay hidden from any passersby. The mountains are inhospitable, but there are some who dwell within parts of them. There are also those that simply wish to reach their peaks for amusement. Secrecy will be important. A magician called Ranalin has guarded the temple for ages and should still watch over it. Our communications seem to be impeded, but he was once a very wise and proficient practitioner.

"We will aim to send you as near to the Power Keep as possible, but as you know, attempting this kind of magick has become unpredictable as of late. I could use your help." Omnicus walked over to the mirror that hung a few feet away.

"Reveal," he said as he looked into it. After a few short moments, the mirror no longer showed the reflection of the room but something different entirely. "This is where we need to send you. These are the gates to the Power Keep. Knya, you know what to do, hmm, hmm. Madden, I'm showing you this so you may help us. Now you see where we mean to send you and you can help us with the magick. I will handle most of the locating, but you can share your energy to increase the strength of the spell. You have done stupendously thus far." Omnicus looked at them with hopeful eyes as night covered the island.

"Okay, are you all ready, my heroes?" he asked. The four companions all looked at one another and nodded as they stood close. "Here we go," Omnicus said.

The great elephant then knelt on the floor. His eyes and tusks began to glow with a golden light as a wind stirred in the hall. Knya spread her arms and the gem around her neck flashed with sparks of violet that spun and surrounded them all.

"Madden, gather your energy. Let it build and then release it. Lend it to us and let our power become one. Let it sweep through you and each of us," Omnicus instructed.

Madden did as he was told and his horn came aglow with colorful light. A moment later, a small space in the air in front of them began to warp and spread. Light clusters ignited and outlined a rift that stretched large enough for each of them to pass through. One by one, they all entered.

10

An Evil Plan

The flying creature, which they had all been puzzled to identify, continued to soar east, away from the mountaintops of Mythras. It was no bird or natural beast. Flapping hard against the ocean wind, eight wings extended from its burly physique, each displaying dull charcoal-black feathers and attaching in pairs to the heels of the animal's four clawed appendages. Thick quills covered its body, but its wide face had slight human characteristics. The creature also dripped a dark sludge while riding the swift currents and galloping through the mist and clouds.

As it soared away from the island, a large shadow formed in the distance just ahead of it. The creature flew straight into the swirling blackness and vanished, only to emerge miles away. It had created a doorway to shorten its travel.

Heading toward dark cliffs and into fog, the creature plunged, diving straight down toward a rocky edge. Just when collision seemed imminent, the creature exhaled, shrank to half size and slipped into a slim crevasse hidden in the tundra.

Dodging sharp ridges and stalactites, it proceeded to fly through a small tunnel in the mountain wall. A shallow stream flowed at the bottom of the tunnel, which then became a ravine and fell abruptly as the shaft opened to reveal a great hollowed fortress.

When the creature reached the clearing, a dim firelight crept up from below. As it slowly descended, the shape of the beast began to shift. Its front legs grew shorter and its claws became hands and feet. Wings and feathers shrank and shriveled into the new form that now resembled a man. As his feet touched down, the shape-shifter quickly fell to the rocks, gasping for air.

He was thick-jawed, with a broad, sharp forehead and primitive nose, apish with hair over most of his body. A tarry grey-black liquid leaked everywhere from his head to his toes.

From out of the shadows emerged several slender creatures around three feet tall that looked like large red salamanders but stood upright and had heads and necks that appeared vaguely simian. Their strange forms were the result of some past magickal tampering, and they too were drizzled with the oily liquid. They frantically scurried toward the shapeshifting being and covered him with a cape, croaking in their amphibious voices. They could speak, but it wasn't English or any language of the modern era. It was an ancient dialect—the language that the shapeshifting being had used in millenniums past before teaching it to these creatures, his urodelan creations. Though, through some sorcery of his, when the shapeshifter chose for a listener (or reader) to understand, they did.

"You're here. You're here! You're here!" the slippery

creatures all shouted.

"Quiet! You'll wake the girl," the shapeshifter hissed with a glare. Then he looked to a dim corner in the cave a few feet away. There, lying on the floor, was a small human girl. It was the same ghostly child from the beach. Her hair and skin were still nearly the same ashen color, but in utter contrast, just beneath her epidermis, darkness pulsed through her veins. It was smudged and smeared on her body too. It gathered on her hands and feet and soaked her thin, tattered dress that looked as if it had once been white with pink flowers at the waist. She didn't stir.

The shapeshifter seemed relieved but was still breathing hard. The creatures all quietly bustled about the craggy cave, which featured an uneven dug-out fireplace, a table that was nothing more than a raised area of cave rock with a few scrolls, jars and vials on it, and a similar rocky chair draped with animal pelts. Three yawning tunnels opened opposite the falling water, leading into further chambers. The manlike shapeshifter slowly pulled himself onto the large chair, trembling.

"Some potion. Replenish, replenish. I'll get it! Here it is! Drink, drink! Find it? Find it? The one?" the creatures all asked.

"Silence! Bring me the mixture!" the shapeshifter growled. They did as he commanded and brought him a small glass bottle filled with a strange liquid. After he drank it down, his breathing slowed, and his strength returned.

"I found nothing, but I was close. I felt it. With each one that becomes mine, the power grows. Yet, there is something different about this one... what, I know not.

The first was young, naïve and still an incredible rival. I took it narrowly. But with its power joined to mine, the others have each become less difficult to collect. The power is at its greatest here in this primordial dark place. Its aid keeps the unicorns in my command and bonds their magicks to me. When I am far, the power wanes from me, and I must return to consume it again. But from here, sending one to do as I command gains precious time for my convalescence.

"I too am aware of what lies within that great peak. I've cast spells all over that mountain to keep any from the weapon, for even I cannot destroy or wield the crown's magick. I've scoured the landscape, as I know they will seek it out. But I will acquire the final unicorn and complete my ritual before they may reach it," the shapeshifter said. He slammed his fist on the rocky arm of his chair, sending a crack slivering through the structure as it echoed throughout the cavern.

"Ah, this vexes me almost as much as the vermin we fight—those plundering murderers. The minds of man—poisoning this fragile paradise with waste and war. It is a very old seed sown long ago within their kind that has ultimately been this planet's slow demise. Homo sapiens, the bloodsuckers.

"They have become vampires upon the earth. Greedy gluttons. Like a virus, they multiply and consume. They have become a sickness and will soon be removed. I can feel the earth aching as they drain her. They must be cleansed, washed away, and the earth fertilized anew with something worthy. Something that doesn't so blatantly disrespect the magick that is life and will hold its true power dearly, desperately.

"My precious tribe, all of them gone when I awoke. Driven past the brink by human evil. They will pay. Extinction should be pondered more deeply by this disease of a species. Real magick has been all but forgotten, but I know what must be done.

"This dark rite will be used wisely, only this time to open the passage and take human evil from the earth at once. Their dark hearts will join the outer realm where they belong. They are incorrigible, remorseless, but we will make them see what they have done, and they will suffer. They only sicken and contribute to the land's demise. Humans wish for a merciful, just God and yet they treat the earth and beasts as demons do. What kind of being is this? Living life in the darkness even though they walk in the sunlight. They hold the first female of their kind to be called by the name of Eve, but I have she who will be the last of their kind, anointed by the same name.

"It is for the planet, sacrificing the wicked souls of some for the souls of many to come. As soon as the task is complete, I will banish the darkness as I have summoned it. We have all but one unicorn left to grasp," he rambled to himself.

Then the sound of shattering glass interrupted his thoughts. His head darted in the direction of the crash. One of the salamander creatures stood in front of a broken vial with a panicked expression. He immediately began cleaning the mess. The girl's eyes flew open. They weren't the empty black they had been. The opaque, impenetrable darkness was now a misty grey that appeared to have some life.

"Aahhh!" Her scream filled the cave. She turned her

head back and forth as if she couldn't quite get a view of anything in the dim firelight. She squinted and waved her arms and felt her face and eyes. "Hello? Is anyone there? Something's wrong with my eyes! I can't see anything," she called out, beginning to weep.

The shapeshifter walked toward her slowly. He lifted his arm, and a twisted branch of a staff floated over to him. He raised it and began speaking an incantation. As he did, the oily liquid that stained her began to flow and swell. It snaked over her body and into her eyes and mouth until she was completely covered. The final words of the spell floated from his wide jaws and the liquid settled. The girl stood lifeless again. The misty grey color of her eyes had now faded to a deep, dark emptiness and she wore no expression.

"Go, perform these tasks with which I charge you," the shapeshifter ordered. The sound of hooves against hard stone crept from out of the shadows as a large fiendish unicorn stepped forward, and the ghostly girl mounted the beast. "Bring me the unicorn."

Together the bewitched beings turned, and both vanished into the shadows of the cave.

"Soon. All but one... then rid of them forever," the shapeshifter babbled, speaking in circles to himself and the devout creatures that waited upon him.

Then the fire slowly diminished until there was no light. All of the amphibious creatures scampered out of the cave, into the dimly lit tunnels. The hissing of the fire's dying embers became a whisper and then a full choking voice.

"BARGAINERRRR ... I FEEEL THE ENERGY. IS IT COME TO PASSS SOON?" the voice seeped.

The shape-shifter took a deep breath. "I have been expecting you. We have but one unicorn to find and the doorway can be opened," he responded.

"**GETTT THE UNEECORNSSSS**," the strained voice replied.

"And our terms, they remain? The souls of man will be payment enough? And you will leave me and the creatures of magick to my precious paradise when you have acquired them all?"

"**YESSSSS. USE THE EEENERGY. COLLECT THE UNEECCCORNSS. OPEN THE DOOOR AND YOU WILL REIN SUPREEME. FREEEEE OF MAN FOREVERR. YOUR POWWERR WILL BECOME INNNFINITE AND YOU CAN NURRRTURE YOUR EARRTH AND HEAL IT AGAAIN.**

I SSSSWEAR IT. I AM VAASSST. I AAMM THE INNFINITE

I AAMMM THE DDAARRRKK

I AAMMM

11

Make for the Mountain

They were all caught by surprise as reality around them jolted, jumped and became distorted. They were whirled into vertigo and only felt stable again as they crashed to the sparse forest floor. Something was wrong.

"Is everyone okay?" Torque managed, collecting himself. They all nodded and grumbled that they were fine.

"What happened?" Madden asked.

"I think something—or someone—must have tried to block us. There was counter-magick interfering," Knya said, looking about, trying to make sense of their location.

All around them were rocky peaks, and a morning sun sent pockets of warmth through a chilly wind. Knya cast a few revelation charms to measure how far they were from their desired objective, incorporating the key as an added directive, being it was anchored to the Cosmite.

"There, the glister above that ridge, it's got to be the gates." She pointed in the distance to an adjacent peak. "We're not where we should be, but we can still make it." They pulled themselves together and hiked toward the incline as the tips of the great mountain range crept upward.

"Careful, Knya! You almost squished me." Torque jumped out of Knya's satchel and flew onto Madden's horn. "We wouldn't want any unpleasant episodes, now would we?"

"I'm sorry, Your Highness, you're absolutely right," Knya mocked.

"What do you mean?" Madden asked.

"Oh, nothing for you to be concerned about, boy." He cleared his throat. "Uh, we all have our demons, that's all."

"Some more severe than others," Knya smirked.

"Yes, indeed," Torque said, stretching his wings. "Argh, I feel as though I have aged an accelerated amount during this adventure."

"Oh, that's just part of *my* trick to stay young... taking youth from you!" Knya said with a laugh.

"Oh, I believe it!" Torque responded giggling. Madden and Braelok laughed too.

When they had progressed a few miles and the gates of the temple became distinguishable, they noticed an immense stone statue placed a few yards off the trail. It was a gnarled and twisted figure of two men conjoined in several places, their heads separated only enough to recognize that their faces were certainly two. Both wore agonizing expressions with open mouths.

"It's so macabre." Madden shuddered.

"There are old tales about two powerful brothers that were born conjoined. In one version, they eventually ended up killing and consuming one another, fighting for their own dominance over the appendages they shared. They didn't realize that in order for one of them to thrive, they both had to thrive. But that's not the version I like. Another version, just as old as the first, is that the brothers did learn this most important lesson, and in doing so they found nirvana in existence and created a beautiful world. I think it is a commentary on our own connection with everything else throughout this earth. Old fables, both of them, but these lessons are just as important today. We can see the theme exercised in art throughout history. Case in point," Torque explained as they all looked the statue over.

"But what about when animals kill other animals?" Madden asked.

"This is true. For as long as we know, the darkness has been among us. But animals mostly kill for survival. As sentient beings, we have been enlightened, shown knowledge, and can choose to do wicked things or not. We are no longer like the animals of the forest in that way, and whether we like to acknowledge it or not, it comes with responsibility. As you've heard, many believe there is a balance that must be maintained. And when that balance is tampered with or the darkness swells, we are the ones who have been given the gifts to fight it. We will all answer for what we've done on this earth."

"Darkness... So you mean a black cat crossing my path is actually bad?" Madden said.

"Oh utter nonsense," Torque replied. "We must never confuse pigment with perniciousness, hue with the horrible. What we are referring to is the absence of light and the evil things that lurk within."

They stepped past the carved stone and continued on

their course.

After another mile the ground beneath them grew steeper. They all began to feel weary as the air grew colder and thinner and each step became heavier and more difficult. A layer of stratus clouds slid sluggishly across the sky and covered the sun, casting an ominous shade on everything. Torque crawled back into Knya's satchel and got cozy. The others decided to rest on a group of rocks and catch their breath.

As they rested, Madden surveyed the vast landscape. Even through the shade and gloom, the view from this height was fantastic. He looked back to his friends, who were huddled, trying to stay warm in the brisk air, and he was thankful for them. They had been through much in a short time. Being chased by wakeful nightmares through the depths and heights of the earth, and they were still going. He admired their strength and bravery and was surprised by his own. The pleasant moment of gratitude lasted another full minute but then quickly fell away, interrupted as something stirred in the furthest corner of Madden's vision. He raised his head to focus just above them on the mountainside and his breath immediately left him. Knya's eyes darted to see what he beheld.

"Not again. Alright, everybody—we're going to have to run," she said almost in a whisper as she stared at the evil approaching. It was another demon unicorn, this one as frightful as the others. Bones punctured through its malnourished body and rotted flesh swung back and forth around its neck. It had hell in its eyes and they knew its malevolent intent. Then they saw another, and then another, each just as mangled as the last and all dripping darkness.

Madden, Braelok, and Knya, with Torque in her satchel, all turned to race from the horrific creatures. Madden didn't make it a few steps before a fourth wraith unicorn appeared from behind a boulder, separating him from his fleeing friends. He froze as the phantom headed straight for him. He was terrified, but there was no time.

He lowered his horn as it lit up, and he willed the beast away from him. Its broken hooves thrashed the air as it reared, but it continued forward again with its head held low. The stiletto points of their horns were now only a few feet from one another. Madden pushed harder and the creature stopped, rearing once more. It was just enough time for Madden to slip past and run for his life as the dark unicorns raced after him. He saw Knya in the distance and galloped toward her.

"Where's Braelok?" Madden asked when he had caught up, skidding to a halt.

"He was right behind me," Knya replied. They glanced around quickly but Braelok was nowhere in sight. "Madden we have to move!"

"Get on!" Madden said. He knelt for a split second while she grabbed his mane and swung up on his withers. He thrust with all his might and jumped back to a gallop, racing away with the shadows of the phantoms close on his heels.

Torque emerged from Knya's satchel to witness the evil that followed. "Oh, my! Run, boy!" he shouted. He jumped from the satchel and opened his wings to the wind.

There were too many of them, and Madden began to feel that strange grabbing feeling again, beckoning and pulling. No matter how fast he ran, he couldn't get far enough, but he

kept steady feet as he raced from the eerie baleful creatures.

Knya acrobatically swung her legs to reverse her position and face the charging specters. She raised her hands above her head and brought them together in a booming clap that sent a shock wave of luminescent atoms exploding toward the pursuers. The dark unicorns reared and threw their heads as they slowed momentarily, but they quickly recovered their speed.

Knya lifted her hands again, clasped them together hard and sent another blast booming toward the dark figures. "They're running right through everything I throw at them," she said as she swung her legs back around and held tightly to Madden's neck and mane.

"I can't outrun them!" Madden's voice flew away fast in the passing wind. "I have an idea, but I don't know if I can do it." Just as the words left his mouth, Madden's horn began to flicker. He envisioned what he needed the magick to do and asked, begged, commanded it to obey him. Then the light from his horn spread about his body and his muscular shoulders began to shine and inflate.

"Madden?" Knya questioned as tiny white specks of fluff sprouted from all over his growing appendages. The fluff grew and fanned out, revealing beautiful, elegant gold-and-white feathers. The feathers stretched up and spread toward the sky until the unicorn boy boasted large impeccable wings grander than the most beautiful swan or eagle.

"My goodness," Torque marveled. Madden's wings began to flap and great gusts of wind swirled beneath his fast-racing hooves. Harder and faster he bade the wings to beat, for trouble not only followed but now lay ahead as well.

As the path came to an end and a great cliff threatened to claim his hard-paced gallop, Madden held his breath and jumped with all the strength that his legs could manage.

Time felt as if it stood still and they were frozen in that moment, in that decision he had made in order to save himself and his friend. He had been able to manifest wings, but was the magick strong enough? And had he acted in time? Would he be responsible for their demise after everything they had been through? They fell quickly, plummeting straight down toward a bed of jutting rock.

12

The Cosmite

Knya and Madden both screamed as gravity heaved at them. She squeezed her arms around his neck and held on for dear life as Torque soared down at their side.

"Madden, wings? How did you—uh, flap! And don't fight the wind! Use it!" he cried.

Through the calamity, Madden tried to apply the dragosaur's coaching. He flapped hard and tried not to fight the incredible currents of air. Yet, in spite of his efforts, the ground was near, and they were speeding toward it. Fatality was yards away and rushing them. Grappling with his distress, Madden steadied his wings, feeling for the currents. He felt a dip and then a wave, and he leaned into it. As they approached the deadly rocks, close enough to see the lichens that grew upon them, his wings caught the great updraft and they were lifted high above the horizon. He had done it. He had willed wings to appear and carried them away from the creatures that threatened them.

"Madden, you're flying!" Knya said.

"Way to go, chap!" Torque called.

"What did you... how did you do that?" Knya questioned in bewilderment.

"Well... It was kind of like the leaf, only... bigger. I think being scared half to death helped," Madden huffed.

But now, how to *really* control these new wings? He flapped and they rose. Gusts from the north pushed and pulled at him as they soared over the mountain. *Don't fight the wind—use it*, he thought to himself again. He calibrated his strong wings and sailed over the currents with more ease as he got the hang of it. Torque followed behind them effortlessly.

As Madden flew, a brief smile grew on his unicorn face, knowing that his magick had succeeded, but worries about Braelok quickly replaced his delight.

"We have to find Braelok," Madden said.

"We'll go back for him but look, there! That's the temple. Can you make it?" Knya pointed to the beacon. "We'll find him and be better off once we get to the Cosmite."

"She's right. We'll search for him when we accomplish what we came to do," Torque said.

Madden reluctantly agreed, knowing they were right, but he was unable to shake his concern for Braelok. He gauged the target and, wings beating staunchly, adjusted their course, aiming toward the temple, breathing hard. Turning into a rough spot of air, the feat became more difficult, and Madden struggled to manage. The winds that they maneuvered through increased in an erratic manner. Madden, only a first time flyer, was beginning to find it impossible to remain steady. The tussle only progressed, and the three

them were soon tossed like jetsam on rough waters, barely able to stay aloft, when the clouds above them began to swirl into motion. The formerly flat indistinguishable blanket of misty clouds was collecting, concentrating over the space that Madden, Knya and Torque flew, turning into a wild merciless storm, thickening into darkness. Knya held on as tight as she could but wasn't able to avoid squealing in distress while they flailed through the calamity. Jerked about, thrown through loops and frightened, Madden did all he could to navigate, but his breathing grew strained.

First one feather, then another and another, came loose from his wings, floating away in the wind. As more and more floated away, Madden and Knya lost altitude.

"Madden! Your wings!" Knya shouted.

"Knya, I don't feel so good," Madden muttered.

"Madden, just focus and try to get us to the ground," she said as she clung to him. Torque fought to swoop closer.

"You've exhausted yourself, boy, but try to hold on, just a little longer," he said. But hundreds of the golden feathers flew into the air and Knya and Madden again plunged toward the mountain below.

The swirling clouds continued to take form, growing into a funnel that then reached down from the heavens and engulfed them. The forces within were just too intense, and Knya was wrenched from Madden's back as the last of the feathers floated from his shoulders. They all shouted to one another, but were all hopelessly separated, pulled apart and sent windborne, hurling in different directions.

Spiraling down fast and suddenly alone, Knya reached

for the gem on her necklace, placed it over her heart and whispered into the wind.

"Ventis... Ventis exaltas me," she repeated again and again, and upon nearing the ground, the wind that had been so cruel swept beneath her and slowed her descent. Knya held tight to her pendent and continued reciting her words, bracing for a rough landing. She came down hard onto a thick patch of scraggly shrubs, but the wind that she had turned in her favor had kept her safe.

Madden tried to push out any magick he could to keep from slamming onto the earth beneath him, but he was spent. He had no energy left to call upon. Nearly worn out and fraught with dread, Madden closed his eyes and gave in to the foreboding thought that he wasn't going to make it. He was scared, but he was angry that he was to fail this way. That he had decided to use the spell that he did. That nature had allowed this uncanny storm to come into manifestation as it had, so abruptly, and so menacingly. These were the only brief thoughts he was granted as he sped toward the firmament. But when he had nearly come to meet it, the wind cradled him too, impeding his fall and setting him down roughly on a growth of twiggy bushes.

He lay there catching his breath and his wits, in utter discombobulation.

Torque had been hurled down in his own direction, but managed to stay airborne after the struggle with the cyclone. When he had gained his bearings, he was able to catch a glimpse of where Knya had landed. He flew to her, distraught with worry. He glided to her side as she stiffly pulled herself to her feet. The storm had mellowed slightly but was still howling around them, throwing dust and jostling the little vegetation that was present.

"Are you alright?" Torque asked with combined anxiety and relief.

"I think so," Knya responded, shaken. "But, Madden, we have to find him. We have to make sure..." She didn't finish her sentence. "Madden?" She called, turning in a circle to listen before calling again. She trembled, overwhelmed with concern.

"I couldn't see where he ended up. But we'll find him," Torque said. "He can't be far." But neither of them mentioned their apprehension in considering Madden's state of wellbeing.

"First Braelok, now Madden... Everything is a terrible mess," Knya said, tears welling in her eyes.

"We have to keep moving. Are you well enough?" Torque said. Knya swallowed and nodded. "Do you have a spell to find which direction Madden is in?"

Knya considered the question, and then plucked a short pearlescent hair that was caught on her clothing before nodding again. She held the tiny hair in one hand and her pendent dangled from its chain in her other. When she spoke the incantation and outlined a few shapes in the air with her fingers, the pendant lifted to point the way.

After a few minutes without movement Madden managed to lift his head.

"Knya? Torque?" he yelled through the wind. There was no answer. He yelled for them again, but heard no reply and saw no one in the vicinity.

Questions arose in his mind. *How had he survived? If he*

didn't call for the cradle of wind, and Knya wasn't anywhere near, who did? It couldn't have been natural, could it?

Madden rolled upright and forced his legs to lift himself. He was frail but regaining some of his strength. He tried to interpret his position in regards to the temple, but he was completely lost. He stood in a slightly slanted plot of valley among sparse hemlock and pine trees, between two ridges towering a hundred yards across from each other. The valley curved above and below him, hiding what lay ahead in either course. He stepped out of the tangling of brittle branches and deliberated on what route he should attempt to embark to find his friends and the weapon.

The ridges were far more treacherous to scale so his only real choices were to take the incline of the valley or to head lower. He decided to take the chance that climbing higher up the slanted ground might bring him closer to the temple and perhaps his friends, if they had also continued toward it, or at least give him a vantage point of view to make sense of where he had landed.

He shook off a few twigs and leaves and proceeded to march upward through the turbulent winds when a sudden wild swirl of sooty grey clouds coalesced and touched down in front of him, further stirring up the land and trees that surrounded.

Madden halted where he stood and the cyclone was equally stationary. Madden slowly took confounded, careful steps backward and then he heard a voice slither into his ears.

"I can see you, child. I can see your true form. But it is of no matter. The power is in you and now it is mine," the voice leaked from the tower of mist as its size began to shrink.

The swirl compacted smaller and smaller until it was the height of a man, and gradually, distinct human features became perceptible– almost human. It was Danuk in the flesh, and the grim girl stepped out from behind him.

"Madden!" Knya shouted out below them, running up the incline just in time to glimpse the scene, with Torque flying beside her.

Madden's horn came aglow while he pivoted to dart from the apish warlock. He bolted into a gallop, finding the little might that he had left. His friends were so close, striding to meet him. He had nearly made it to join them again, but Danuk cast his magick with swiftness.

An oily projection sprang from the dark warlock and swept under Madden's footing, causing him to falter, grappling at him, pulling him down into the negative caliginous space the puddle had created, until he sank entirely. Then the puddle diminished to nothing, returning to firm earth.

Knya screamed and fell to her knees at witnessing what had happened. She called out a spell with furious passion, and aiming to kill, thrust her hands in front of her, sending the most potent glaring discharges of colorful light she had ever produced rocketing toward Danuk.

Danuk grinned smugly and held out his hand. When Knya's magick approached he grasped it into an orb, and holding its bright energy, he called his darkness forth, covering the light with opaque shadow, until it disappeared completely. An orb of oily fog was all that remained and he cast it back toward her, reaching his mark perfectly, splashing it across her face and chest. Torque flew forward and was approaching the warlock, ready to breath flames, but as he came in range, pushing out searing fire, Danuk and the deathly girl sank into a dark puddle of their own that quickly swallowed itself up, just as the puddle that swallowed Madden had. The blustery weather settled almost immediately after the villainous pair had vanished.

There was nowhere to follow. Torque flew back to Knya's aid. The dark ooze that covered her obstructed her breathing. They both tried tearing it from her face, but it had become solid, clinging to her. They panicked, knowing each second was critical to Knya's survival. She was losing color when, unexpectedly, the darkness began to bubble below her collar. It was liquefying again and then it started to drip away. It slid from her chest to reveal the magick key, shining as if it had been heated to extreme temperatures, and the recession continued until all of the ooze had evaporated. Knya gasped for air.

"Oh thank heaven! The key! It must have some magick of its own. Are you okay?" Torque said.

"I'm okay," Knya replied with tears in her eyes. "But what do we do? This is exactly what we were supposed to prevent. We were supposed to protect him!"

"All is not lost! We have to get to the Cosmite. Then we can still save him. Have you strength enough for another revelation spell to get us to the temple?"

Knya sat up and tried to calm herself. Then she cast the charm they required. Fortune smiled on them in that small moment. They were closer to the temple than they imagined and they rushed toward it immediately.

They didn't spare a second, and after negotiating an

unfavorable route under a clearing sunny sky, they soon came to the gates of the Power Keep. Huge and secure, the imposing plates were set a few feet into the side of the mountain, with intricate carvings reaching over the length of them. Some of the carvings were of humans, some animals, and some seemed to have a sequence and tell a story. Blemishes and scars of ages also adorned the massive structures of the entrance, and fallen rock and windswept debris piled in front of the gates, obscuring their appearance. The mineral from which they were forged had become tarnished, but it still had a unique luster. Torque climbed onto Knya's shoulders.

"Do we knock?" Knya wondered aloud.

Torque shrugged. "Seems polite," he said.

Knya tried to knock as hard as she could on the dense slabs. It nearly made no sound at all and only caused her to worry she might have broken her knuckle.

"Knya, if you can just get the doors opened a bit, we can slip inside," Torque suggested. Knya took a deep breath and stared hard as she made a strained grasping gesture. With a tiny glimmer of her pendant, the huge gates began to tremble, but they wouldn't budge.

"They're too strong," she said, breathing heavily. "There has to be a way to get in."

"I'm sure they're protected by magick, but what kind?" Torque said, looking the enormous gates over. "Perhaps we are missing something."

They turned to the right of the gates and looked for any sign. Torque flew above for any aerial indication. When they had gone several yards, they turned back and passed to the left of the gates. After a few steps, they both noticed a crumbled depression in the rocky wall. It didn't seem like much and could have easily been mistaken for an ordinary formation in the structure. Torque flew over to the crevice to search for any clues. He landed on some loose sediment, and as it fell they glimpsed something that looked like writing.

They cleared the remaining obstruction to reveal a small, hollowed space that was surely no natural construct. It measured about a foot tall, a foot wide, and two feet deep, with carvings of vines in a diamond shape at the back. A blue gemstone was lodged in the center of the vines with small writing just below it. Above the stone rested a carved symbol that looked like a half-sun, half-moon. Knya stepped closer.

"Torque, can you read that?" she asked.

Torque gave it a deciphering look. "I think it says... 'Use the light'." They looked out at the sky as the sun sank lower on the horizon. "Can you catch any of that sunlight and shine it directly at the stone?"

Knya adjusted her pendant until she reflected the last bit of setting sunlight where he instructed. For a few moments, nothing happened. But after just a few more, the doors shifted, sliding open.

They cautiously stepped past the opening as a damp, stale breeze floated out. It was dark and quiet inside. Knya illuminated her gem and they each tried to get a view of what lay around them. To their surprise, the stone walkway was only a few feet long. It was as if the gates opened into a narrow cave that ended almost where it began. They both looked it over as well as they could.

"Maybe there is a passage or another door?" Torque flew about, investigating.

"Or maybe the place has completely caved in," Knya said. They examined the walls, searching for anything. Knya lifted her hand to feel the flow of the air and followed it to the back of the cave.

"There is a tiny hole here with a breeze coming out of it... I wonder if it means anything?" She brought her face close to the opening to get a better look.

Then suddenly Knya screeched and fell backward as her body stiffened. Torque followed and landed next to her. They were both paralyzed. The tiny hole in the cave grew as the rocks crumbled away and a human-looking old man emerged from the dust and shadows. Scraggly white hair fluffed around the crown of the man's head, continuing down his face into a short white beard, and his skin was the color of cinnamon. About his body he wore a tattered, loose, brown robe that dragged on the floor with each step he took. His hands glowed blue-hot with fire, and he placed one of them along the rough cave wall.

"Stiff as stone, stiff as stone," he whispered as he approached. "Who dares trespass here? Did you think you would catch me in slumber? Arrogance! I have not let a single sneak thief pass this hall in all my service!" A booming voice came from the magician, who was controlling them with a powerful magick.

"We're from Eloria... Omnicus sent us," Torque managed through clenched teeth.

The magician paused and looked them over, still holding his spell tightly. He took a breath and dropped his hand from the rocks, releasing Knya and Torque. Both of them gulped for air. Knya reached for the key around her neck and held it out in her hand. The magician came closer and stared at the brass piece.

"Oh my. Well, I'll be... Omnicus? That elephant lad? Well, why did you not say so sooner? I suppose it is about time you got here."

With a wave of his hand, the narrow cave shifted. Stones rolled away as it widened, revealing a wonderfully lit spacious hall with thick carved pillars, a hard stone floor and a hearth burning in the distance. Torque and Knya pulled themselves up. The old magician was very chatty as he led them past where rugged walls had once been, and they all entered the temple. He and Knya's footsteps echoed in the large chamber while Torque flew.

"Well, you must know I am Ranalin the Guardian. Come on, follow me, don't dawdle. Now, I am sorry for the way I greeted you, but things have been a bit off-putting lately, and I have a job to do. There were once many here, educating others and protecting this power. Now I am the only one left. If I do say, I have felt the sting of loneliness up here, and possibly more severely as of late. I have not had *any* kind visitors in some time, and magick only continues to be forgotten little by little. But I will not stop. I still send birds with messages to the other communities. Call me old-fashioned. But most don't even truly realize what power is being kept here. And in all this time, there has been nobody quite right for the job to replace me. Nobody with the right strength in the power or the heart like there used to be. By human standards, I have endured through numerous lifetimes, and I had to continue in order to find someone to protect this place when I parted."

162

"You've done a most incredible job, Ranalin," Torque offered. "Through your efforts, you have aided us all."

"The one we face... he's using unicorns, changing them, putting dark curses on them to do his evil, to perform a dark ritual that would decimate the earth," Knya said. "We think he means to acquire eight in total, and now he may have them all."

Ranalin paused. "I have seen many extraordinary things in my time... but I have met very few unicorns. How did he come to possess so many of them? Imagine the power, if he knew how to use it. I have been feeling all kinds of strange energy lately that shouldn't be swarming around. I knew that things were off. I suppose I did not want to rush to dire conclusions. Only a few nights past, something came to the temple. Something dark. It somehow crossed the gates and made it into the hall. I battled it with all my might. It was more than formidable. Stronger than anything I've felt for a long time. Using the powers of this place I stopped it from advancing and I sent it on its way, but the whole thing shook me. It was intense. I swore not to leave my post, but I began to worry. I even had thoughts to try and wield the crown myself. Foolish. It is not meant to be worn by anyone but who it's meant for... I couldn't have gotten to it if I wanted to anyhow," the old wizard said.

"He was here on the mountain, only just before we arrived at these gates. He took our friend, a boy who was foreseen by the oracles and has become a unicorn. We have to get the crown to this boy. He may be the only one who can unleash its power," Knya urged.

"My word," Ranalin said.

163

They continued through the temple, turning corners that brought them into new areas that looked exactly like the last. It was a maze of pillars and huge rooms that mirrored each other until finally a large, arched golden door appeared. Ranalin led them toward it and unlocked it with a key of his own. He pulled the door open, and what they saw within took their breath away.

A room of colorful light unfolded before them. It swelled and swayed as every hue floated around like a million prisms had caught the sun. They entered and immediately felt bliss and joy. There were no walls, no constraints. The light went on forever around them. Knya gripped the key and a few seconds later the box appeared. It was made of a shining metal. It looked like platinum or lightest gold. Inscriptions adorned each of its sides, and Knya knew that the writing was magickal: powerful protection spells of the ancient. The box floated above them and slowly descended just in front of her. She stepped closer with the key in hand. She slowly placed it in the small hole on the front of the box and turned. The top lifted and they peered inside. It was empty.

"I don't understand," Knya said, looking to Ranalin.

And then a flicker and a spark erupted from within the box. A flame brighter than the light that surrounded them spouted in a circular shape. It looked like a royal crown of colorful fire. It was the Cosmite. They all stared in wonder for a few moments before Knya closed the box.

"We have to go. There's no time to waste," Knya said to them.

"Now, wait just one moment! I have looked after that thing for longer than you have been in existence. You cannot just take it out of here... not without me too," Ranalin said.

"Then we will all take it to Eloria, and together we will find a way to save Madden and defeat Danuk's wild plan," Torque said.

"And what did you suppose you were going to do? Walk all the way back the way you came?" Ranalin asked.

"We have to get there any way we can. Immediately. Madden needs us and we need him! Do you think together we could make a passage to the city?" Knya asked the elder magician.

"Well, that is exactly what I think we ought to try," he said.

He led them out of the room of light and down a series of corridors until they came to a hall with large double wooden doors at the end. When they approached the doors Ranalin gestured into the air with his fingers and a glow ignited from them.

"Patentibus," he said and the doors opened.

They entered a sizeable room that seemed to be some sort of library or study with numerous books stacked on a multitude of shelves twenty feet high. A spiraled staircase on the left side of the room reached up to a second level platform and a sliding ladder was available opposite for retrieving the higher placements. A desk with candles, papers, and several hefty ancient-looking volumes splayed upon it sat toward the middle-left of the room, and a few stands with more books on them were placed close by. Glass paned cabinets with vials and jars full of assorted minerals and liquids occupied an area to the rear-right side of the room, and a large silver basin sat near it. A smaller but similar looking cabinet stood at the rear-left side of the room, stocked with what appeared to be unrelated talismans, totems and tokens. A basketball sized sphered gem sat upon a carved wooden base across the room from the desk, just in front of a small hearth that lit as they entered.

"Are these all books on magick?" Knya asked.

"Yes, written and collected by many over the years, although countless others have been lost to tyranny throughout the ages," Ranalin said.

"I think you have more here than the library in Eloria," she said.

"Perhaps you should come back and have a peak at a more opportune time."

"Yes, I'd like that."

Ranalin stepped over to the smaller cabinet and retrieved a petite object that was carved into the shape of a beetle. "This will make the travel easier." Then he produced an imperfect wooden spray of a wand from his robe. "Now, I'll let you direct us. But I'll be pushing. Are you ready?" he asked.

Knya nodded. She began to concentrate and held her gem fast in her hand, igniting it with a twinkle. Ranalin lifted his wand in one hand and the beetle shaped totem in the other, adding his own illumination to the spell. Torque crawled back into Knya's satchel and poked his head out. The light shimmered and glowed brighter about their bodies as the scenery around them changed. Slowly they were taken from inside the walls of the temple to the outskirts of Eloria. It was morning again on the island. As their new coordinates became more opaque, Knya searched their surroundings and saw the Oracle's fortress in the distance.

"Did we make it? Are we completely through?" She

looked down at Torque and then to Ranalin. The spell was slightly different but everyone had traveled safely. They hurried to the castle and were greeted with brief smiles, followed quickly by sadness at the news of Madden's capture.

Omnicus introduced them to two other sorcerers who had journeyed from different parts of the world to lend their support. Zhao Latzu, a master in the study of the ancient magick of Qi, had traveled from Asia, and Andan Ga was the high magician of shamanic traditions from Africa, who had also discovered the location of Danuk's lair. As soon as formalities passed, everyone quickly began discussing what should be done.

"I think stealth is our ally on this mission. Madden and the Cosmite may be the only things that can stop him and this darkness now," Andan Ga said.

"Yes, if we battle him outright with the unicorns at his side, it could mean immense destruction," Zhao Latzu said. "If one of us can enter his lair in secret and free the unicorn boy before he completes his ritual, then Danuk can be stopped. All of the unicorns will be free again, and his terror can be eliminated." Ranalin and Omnicus agreed.

Knya was exhausted between the travel and events of the journey, but she felt committed to continue. "I'll go," she volunteered.

"I'll go with you," Torque said.

"Are you sure you're up to the burden? You've both just returned from a daunting day, only to leave again with no rest," Omnicus reasoned.

"We've come this far," Knya said.

"Yes, this is our task," Torque corroborated.

The company agreed, and they wasted no time. Ranalin approached Knya and held out the small beetle totem in his hand.

"To help you travel," he said. Knya accepted it and thanked him. Then the five sorcerers stood in a circle and cast their magick. An orb of light ignited in the center of their formation, sparking and flaring, expanding and contracting unpredictably. Penetrating the strength of Danuk's defenses challenged the extent of their power, even channeled collectively, but they pressed with all they had, and after a considerable struggle they succeeded in maintaining a small brief rift. Knya and Torque would again be transported to another place and time of day upon the earth. The fluctuating orb of light in the center of the sorcerers stretched and widened until it soon showed a view of the dark, stony room where Madden was held captive.

13

The Rite

Madden came to and lifted his head. He looked around, trying to discern anything he could in the dimness. The floor beneath him was cold and hard. A faint light slowly became visible as his eyes adjusted. He pulled himself to his feet and took a step forward, only to feel and then hear the heavy chain that was dangling from his ankle. Fear struck him as he began to remember sinking into the darkness and realized he was now a captive. Two of the larger urodelan creatures stood in the room on each side of a single wooden door. Other than a few brief side-eyed looks and a croak or hiccup now and then, they remained still while standing guard.

Madden stamped down hard with his chained hoof. The sound echoed and rang out. As it reverberated something else arose into the acoustics. The clinking sound of a wooden staff on stone between slow, uneven footsteps approached from outside the room. The door flew open and revealed a dark shrouded figure on the other side. The figure stepped through the threshold, toward Madden.

"Knya?" Madden said, squinting.

"Ha. You reveal your naivety even now in the face of your adversary. Weakness. Come, are you ready to witness the most important moment in the history of the human species? To be a part of it?" The dark figure pulled back his hood, revealing his primitive face. It was Danuk.

"You're insane. I'll never be a part of it. I'll use every atom of my being to fight it," Madden said. He tried to ease his mind, to focus on gathering his energy, and his horn began to glow.

"Child, I do not feel any regret for human beings. They are simply too problematic, too dangerous, a detriment to all others. They have been responsible for the extinction of countless species. They destroyed all of my kind, and they are destroying the earth. It is only what you call justice. Try as you may to keep me out, you won't. You can't. And nothing, not even the crown, can change what is done once my ritual is complete."

"Yes, humans aren't perfect! We are capable of evil. But most people are good. There is love and compassion too, and they're worth saving. This won't bring your people back," Madden said.

"You are deceived, child. I have you to thank for aiding me. With your transformation, you made my ritual possible. You became exactly what I needed for my plan. This is the way it is supposed to be. Can't you see that?" Danuk smiled.

Madden closed his eyes, staying silent and focused, his horn pulsing with energy. Then he felt another presence in the room... something familiar. He opened his eyes and saw

Braelok stepping through the shadows. But Braelok looked strange. His bright russet-umber eyes were now dark grey, and he seemed mindless, under some spell. Madden gasped.

"Braelok!" he called, but Braelok showed no sign of recognition. Madden sighed. He tried to remember his lessons. He gathered his strength, collecting all he could and then pushed his magick forth.

"Let him go!" Madden shouted as a flare of colorful light discharged from his horn, hurling toward Danuk. The dark warlock reacted in perfect time, tapping the bottom of his staff on the floor, causing a shadowed veil to manifest in front of him, shielding him from Madden's attack as it slammed against it. He cackled while Madden stood winded.

"Ha-ha-ha! Boy, what did you think? A strapping hero just happened along the road precisely at your time of need? Fools, the lot of you! I am of the ages of old magick. The depths and heights will be mine to command. Come and look upon your hero now," the dark warlock said.

With a small wave of his twisted staff, Danuk proceeded to will Braelok like a puppet, taking control of his body, but Braelok's face still told the horror he was experiencing. Madden struggled to garner his energy again as Braelok's feet began to leave the ground and he lifted into the air, appendages spread. Braelok shouted in agony, and then darkness surrounded him. Shadows crept over his body as he began to change. His nose and mouth grew, fur and scales sprouted over his skin, and fangs jutted from his screaming jaws as his physique inflated several times.

A tear streamed down Madden's cheek as he witnessed Braelok's entire form altered into something heinous. The shadows settled and the new form slowly became visible. It was the monstrous chimeric beast from Madden's first encounter with a unicorn. Braelok was the beast.

Madden's heart pounded as he fit the pieces together. The scars on Braelok's body—on the side of his torso and the other on his neck, the stag and the pocketknife—it was all laid in front of him now, and it took his breath away. Madden felt stunned, confused and betrayed, but he knew he had to keep fighting. He closed his eyes and knelt as his horn glowed brighter.

"Awww, life is just full of astonishment, isn't it?" Danuk said, reaching into his cloak and retrieving a small grey gemstone. He lifted it in his palm just in front of Madden, but when he lowered his palm, the gem remained in the air. "The time draws near. You will give in to the dark, and I will return for you."

Danuk and his slave monstrosity turned toward the door, and as they left the room, a swarm of shadows followed. The gem remained in its spot. For a few moments all was quiet. Then the gem commenced to release a fine stream of a caliginous smoky substance, as if a candle were burning under it, but there was no flame. The substance spiraled and filled the room, its darkness advancing and surrounding Madden. It swirled over him, reaching out as if to touch him, yet he remained focused and the light from his horn stayed fast, creating a barrier against the dark energy. But how long could he maintain?

A strange rippling sound brought Madden out of his meditation. He opened his eyes, and through the dark energy floating so close to him, he could see sparks fly from the corner of the stone cell. The sparks grew larger and streamed into a thin, straight line that extended from the floor to the ceiling. Madden wasn't sure what was happening but tried to keep his concentration. He had lost all track of time in the concealed malignant dungeon and was no longer certain of the actual duration of his captivity.

A few seconds later, two bolts of light shot out horizontally from the bright beam, making the guards fall like rag dolls. Two figures then flared out of the illumination, and as the light settled, he saw Knya and Torque. He was so happy to see his friends, but he was exhausted. His focus shifted and the darkness broke through his defense. It encompassed him like a cocoon, and began to shrink in and cover him. Knya screamed and raced toward the floating gem that seemed to be emitting the dark energy. She reached to lift it, but as her hands came within an inch, they began to burn and turn grey. She screamed again, this time in pain.

"That wall, Knya. I can hear the ocean behind it. It's not too thick. Outside the sun is still shining," Torque cried. She turned and pressed her hands against the hard stone surface.

"Separatum! Separatum!" she shouted as the walls shook and cracked. "Separatum!" Smaller and smaller pieces crumbled until tiny grains of sand fell everywhere, letting sunlight pour through the opening. They could see Madden's unicorn figure through the dark cloud surrounding him.

"Now try!" Torque said. Knya whispered another incantation with her opalium stone in hand, and then jumped as hard as she could, coming down with a swift kick. The malignant gemstone flew from its position and shattered into pieces. The darkness cleared like smoke and they ran to Madden's side. He appeared lifeless. His bright shimmering color was now a dull grey. Tears fell from Knya's eyes as she reached out to him.

"Madden? Madden... you have to wake up now," Knya pleaded, but he remained still. She brought his head into her lap and wept while she held him. Torque flew to her side.

"Madden, come on, lad. Come back," he said. Knya took a deep breath and tried to compose herself. The warmth of the sun was fading and as it began to set, Knya began conjuring. Whispering an incantation, her gem sparkled and its light fell upon Madden. Presently, the spectacle continued without any change.

Then she lifted her head and had a thought. She began to sing very quietly through her tears. As she sang, the illumination grew and spread throughout the room, spinning all around them, sparking brighter. Madden remained motionless, but then his horn began to glow too. His body trembled, and dazedly, Madden's eyes crept open.

"Knya?" Madden's voice came softly.

"Oh! My goodness, Madden, I was so scared." Knya exhaled a deep breath of relief.

"What happened to you, boy? Are you alright? He was trying to turn you into one of those monsters. You're all grey!" Torque said, looking him over. Madden lifted his head, blinking hard a few times. He had lost his pearlescent lambency and appeared to be at least fifty pounds thinner.

"I... I don't know. I couldn't see much. I just had horrible, horrible feelings. Terrible rage and fear, pain and sorrow. I don't remember everything. Just an empty, inside-out feeling and... darkness," Madden said with a sigh. "Wait... wait, no... there was something, something else I saw. Like flashes in the dark. Little parts of him. His memories... or plans. Oh!"

Madden gasped as, one by one, more and more flashes came rushing to him. "That little girl. She is only a... host that Danuk has collected. There is a shadow over her. She is a prisoner of his, like the unicorns. And Braelok... Danuk has him under some spell too. He's been changed into some kind of animal," Madden said.

"We'll find him. Can you stand?" Knya asked.

Madden brought himself to his feet and stretched his legs. The chain was still dangling around his ankle. Knya reached for it.

"No, let me," Madden said. He brought his horn to the iron clasp, and with a tiny spark it fell to the stone floor. "How did you get in here? And where is here?" he asked.

"We are in his lair within the dark cliffs, between the coasts of Africa and Madagascar," Knya said. "We were finally able to find it, but we needed a little help. Not even Omnicus and I would have been able to make it into this place on our own. This is way out of my wildest dreams. But with the help of a few other sorcerers, Torque and I made it through. Madden, we brought the crown. We can still stop him."

Madden stepped forward into the setting sunlight. He walked right to the edge of the sand-covered floor where the wall had fallen to grains. The stony cell now opened to the outside world, and he realized that they were on a high cliff, with mist covering the view below. He could hear the distant sound of smashing waves, and far on the horizon, a scarlet ocean gleamed. Night was quickly approaching. Although he had already been through unimaginable circumstances, he knew he was still not finished, but he couldn't stop thinking of Braelok.

He turned to his companions. "I'm ready," he said. He knelt and motioned for Knya to get on his back. She jumped on and they headed for the door. Madden brought his horn to the latch, and with another spark, the door swung open.

The sound of Madden's hooves rang out like a nimble marching snare as he and Knya made their way down the rocky halls with Torque flying behind them. They were halted at a few dead ends and a passageway that gave the impression that it repeated itself over and over, but with each obstruction Madden or Knya felt a sense of the correct direction or saw the magickal seams of a hidden doorway, and they took off again. The urodelan creatures leaped from Madden's path as the trio headed toward the evil.

Then Madden rounded a corner and slid to a stop as the possessed little girl appeared in a corridor leading to the ritual room. She had her head tilted low so that they couldn't see her eyes. When she lifted it, darkness reached out down the hall and covered everything around them. The walls faded away and they could see nothing but the possessed girl. Yet as soon as the darkness grew, so too did the light of Madden's horn and Knya's gem. Torque blew a ring of fire.

"Madden, the crown," Knya said as she reached into her satchel and retrieved the box.

She jumped off of his back, gave him a smile and opened the latch. The crown ignited and reflected in Madden's wide eyes. Knya lifted it from the box and placed it on his horn. It hovered just around the middle of the length of his ivory point. Almost at once, his coat turned pearlescent white again and he felt a phenomenal energy surge through him.

"Do you feel that?" Madden asked. "What is that? It's so... peaceful. Can you feel it?" Knya looked at him, and although she was not experiencing the same thing, she understood what was happening.

"Yeah, I think so," she said. Madden looked at the tattered bewitched girl and then the darkness that surrounded them. The crown flared upon his glowing horn and the walls became visible around them again.

"The Cosmite," Danuk's voice hissed from the ghostly girl. "More resilient than we believed, boy, and now you wield the Cosmite. No matter. You are no longer required. I have already taken the final unicorn. The creature was crossing the white lands of the freezing Arctic, but she is in my collection now. The ritual has begun."

Madden took slow steps toward the small child that was possessed by the apish warlock, and with each one, the darkness crept back.

"What... ha-ha... what are you... doing? No... ssstop..." Danuk's voice began to jump and plunge in its pitch. "The human's treacheries must end. You are the evil ones for protecting their wickedness! It is a sacrifice for existence! I am Gifted Among the Many. I shall be vindicated and reign supreme! You... have... no power... here!" The dark warlock's voice shrieked while the girl's body writhed and her shape warped. Darkness slid off of her like liquid, puddling at her feet and then flowing backward away from her.

When Madden stood right in front of her, the darkness was gone. What remained was no longer the body of a living girl but the radiant light of her soul in a girl's silhouette. Knya and Torque stared in amazement as the radiant girl looked at Madden and smiled.

"My eyes. Thank you," she said. Then she turned her head toward the room behind her. "But I can't stay. Please take care of my brother. The door has been opened. You have to close it." The lucent child gradually lifted into the air and the light of her shape dissipated. Knya and Torque hurried over to Madden.

"Did she mean...?"

"Yes, brother and sister," Madden said and then he turned to walk toward the room where the ritual was being performed. The doors swarmed with shadows, and he felt the energy pulsing from inside. When they came to the entrance, Madden lowered his horn with the crown upon it, and as he stepped forward the shadows retreated. The doors trembled and flew open.

The room was enormous. It was roughly round, with high, uneven walls and no ceiling, except a few protruding rock slabs, the opaque mist-covered night sky visible just beyond them. A low, humming rumble permeated the dank chamber, and a single dim torch hung in a corner. They now saw that the other unicorns were all covered in grey-black ooze, their mangled bodies positioned in a circle around a slightly raised altar. They stood listless and seemed entranced, heedless of the shadows that flew around them.

But above the unicorns, an even more uncanny scene unfolded. A chasm in the fabric of space loomed and swelled in size, stretching out, replacing the visible matter around it with dark emptiness. He had done it. Danuk had opened a wormhole reaching into the deepest recesses of the universe, spanning immeasurably through the architecture of the macrocosm. He had invited the darkness, beckoned it, and it was seeping in. The apelike sorcerer and his monster, Braelok, stood on a small platform at the top of a twisted stone staircase that overlooked the altar. A few large gems were placed among them.

Knya turned to Madden. "You have to go alone, but our magick is with you. You have everything you need. It's up to you now," she said shakily.

"You are an extraordinary creature. Now go save us all," Torque added.

"I think I saw... or got a glimpse of... what I have to do. I just hope it's right," Madden said.

"Great goodness bless us," Knya said, kissing his cheek as a tear slowly streamed down hers. "It's time! Now!"

Madden took a deep breath and reared. He jumped into a gallop and headed straight for the unicorns. As he entered the room, a fierce roar echoed throughout the temple. The bewitched beastly Braelok leapt down from the overlook and was heading straight for him.

"Ha-ha-ha! Have you come to offer your own soul?" Danuk screeched. He lifted his staff and the chasm expanded faster, an abysmal void reaching out in all directions above them.

Knya and Torque watched from the edge of the large room's entrance. She sent blasts of violet light surging toward Braelok, but the dark magick present dwarfed her own.

Continuing her efforts to conjure, she thought she must be fooled by some trick of the shadows. She saw her hands slowly fade and disappear. She was speechless with terror. Danuk's ritual was working.

Madden raced, and with all his might he jumped into the center of the circle of unicorns, onto the altar. The monstrous thing that was Braelok landed just on the other side of the raised space, dripping darkness, with its sabre teeth exposed, ready to destroy. They faced each other for a fleeting instant, and as the thing began to lunge, Madden aimed his horn. The grim monster leapt forward but was halted in midair just a few feet from the unicorn boy. Suspended above the ground, the black sludge began to lift off of the beast's body and dissolve. As the sludge disappeared, the shape beneath it also changed. It shuddered, shrank, and scrunched and slowly started to resemble a human again. Braelok was returning to his form. His body descended to the altar and lay motionless.

Now eight mangled dark unicorns stood symmetrically around a single pearlescent shining one, and a human boy lay at their feet.

"Imbeciles!" Danuk scoffed, waving his staff hard again, causing the temple to quake. The black hole's expansion accelerated as the structure around them threatened to collapse into it.

Tears fell from Madden's eyes onto Braelok's body. "Oh! The light, I can see now. I feel it... so clearly. This is the reason. My love is of the light and its forces are great. I understand the darkness and the light within us all. I give my immortal body and call to the light throughout the far reaches of the universe. Come now and illuminate this darkness. I am an instrument of the bringer of life and love, the light."

Without a moment to spare, Madden lifted his head crowned with the flame and reared. As the darkness surrounded them, Madden's horn erupted with an energy unlike any of them had ever seen. The light grew and poured from his eyes and then from all over his body. Intense photons illuminated outward, pushing back the evil. Torque and Knya looked on at the small luminous creature that stood against the vast, consuming expanse, and progressively they no longer saw the shape of a unicorn but that of another human boy. Danuk's voice screeched from the overlook above.

"No! I have upheld my end of the terms! Release me!" He shouted as the darkness pulled at him and he was lifted into the chasm. His form slimmed and stretched like smoke being pulled by a wind, until he vanished into the emptiness.

The light continued to grow until Knya and Torque both had to shield their eyes from its great intensity. It was as if the sun was in the temple with them—some incredible starlight being channeled through Madden and the Cosmite. Soon, weightlessness took them all, and they drifted from consciousness into a great ocean of peaceful dreams.

14

Dawn

The gentlest breeze roused Madden from the comforts of his slumber. He opened his eyes to soft rays of morning sunlight. The ruins of the hall lay all around him, but most of the rubble seemed to have been forced outward. Madden now looked onto a vast plateau of patchy grass, surrounding a shallow cratered area, dotted with boulders and crumbled rocks. Only a few broken walls of the dark warlock's ritual room remained, the rest returned to the rocky earth. Just beyond the extent of the ruins, the plateau ended abruptly at a steep drop, but the edge of a forest could be seen in the distance.

"Knya? Torque?" Madden called. He glanced around frantically and realized that he had hands and feet. He was human again—and naked. He touched his arms with his fingers and then ran them over his face and forehead. Smooth skin was all he felt, but a small, barely-raised colorless spot remained on his warm olive complexion where his horn had once been. He climbed to his feet and hopped over piles of rubble. He saw a few normal-sized salamanders wriggling toward the forest and then heard a rustling coming from behind a large piece of wall that still stood. Torque's tiny dragosaur head poked from around the side, and Knya followed.

"Madden...? Madden!" Knya shouted. They ran toward him. She covered him with her cape and they embraced. After being a unicorn, he didn't really mind that he was naked, but remembered that as a human, he should. "You did it! And look at you!" Knya said.

"We did it!" Madden said.

"What happened to the Cosmite?" she asked.

"Returned to the energy of existence, from which it was borrowed, and dispersed throughout the universe," Torque said.

"The unicorns are free, and Danuk has gone with the darkness," Madden said.

"Braelok?" Knya asked.

"I don't know..." Madden said, confusion and sadness washing over him. They searched the area, calling for Braelok and hoping for any sign. While they climbed over debris, a glimmer appeared between two rocks and they headed toward it. It was Braelok's sword, but there was still no sign of him. They retrieved the gleaming blade and continued.

"What's that over there?" Torque pointed ahead of them while hovering above. Madden looked to see something that appeared animal lying beneath crumbled wreckage. They approached and realized it was one of the unicorns, its coat still a dull grey color and slicked with the dark liquid.

"Could the wickedness have remained?" Torque said, puzzled.

They removed the crumbled rock from the unmoving body. Madden examined the unicorn closer and began to sense something familiar. Then he saw it. Upon its chest, there was a small star-shaped patch a single shade darker than the rest of its coat. It was the unicorn he had rescued only days before, although now it felt like a lifetime ago. This was the unicorn that had granted him the wish and given him the ability to transform—the gift that had begun this great journey.

Madden knelt and touched his own forehead where his horn had been. The colorless spot began to glow, and then he touched the unicorn's head. The magick swelled with less effort and poured out of him. He felt it strong within himself and he continued to let it flow. The unicorn's body lying on the grass quivered, and slowly, the darkness that covered it evaporated. The sludge dried and cracked away, first from Madden's hand and then down the entire length of the magickal animal's body, floating away like dust in the breeze.

They all stared at the shining creature that had appeared in front of them. The unicorn was now a glowing pearl-white hue, and it began to awaken. They all kept their distance as it stood and composed itself. It took a step and looked out at all of them standing around.

"I thought I might never emerge from that darkness. I imagined I had spent an eternity there, yet now I am returned and the earth has not aged. This is twice thou hast saved me, Madden, but thou hast done so much more. Truly, thou art an exceptional being. In honesty I was sent to keep a watch upon thee, but fortune has smiled upon me to meet thee each time as I have. And I thank thee dearly," the unicorn said.

"Thank you for granting me that wish. It's done more

for me than I would have ever known... and I could never have imagined I'd actually be able to help so many others too. I'm more than thankful," Madden said.

The unicorn bowed its head. As he did, Madden noticed movement at the edge of the clearing. Seven unicorns stepped out of the flora and stood next to one another. To Madden's surprise, their coats were all unique: three were the familiar pearly-white, one a deep chestnut with a light sandy mane, another was dappled grey, one had brown and white patches and one was solid sable. They were all shining and restored to health. Each lowered its head to bow. Madden turned to make sure Knya and Torque were seeing what he was. They both nodded and smiled. Madden then turned back and returned the unicorns' bow.

"I am called Stellumar by those who use such names. If ever thou needst aid, look for me in the land of Kero Emagus," the unicorn with the star shape said. And just as it had done when it had met Madden the first time, it reared as it turned to gallop away. They all watched as the unicorns sparkled in the sunlight and disappeared into a shimmer. Madden smiled as he caught the last glimpse.

When the unicorns had gone the trio proceeded their search of the area, covering the grounds three times over, overturning fragments, using magick to lift the heavy boulders, and calling out, vigilant to find any trace of the boy with whom they had been through so much.

"Do you think he could have... survived?" Madden asked. Knya and Torque both paused.

"I pray that he did," Knya said.

"It might not be an easy thought, but it could also be

186

possible that he already left and started on his own tasks," Torque said. Madden turned away, grappling with his emotions. They were all quiet for a minute.

"I have an idea," Knya said, and she set to trying a location spell, casting it with Braelok's image in her mind, noting that it would have been much easier if she had a piece of his hair or a drop of his saliva. Yet, after working through some difficulty she held out her necklace and let the pendent dangle. It twiddled ordinarily for a few seconds before it started to favor a particular direction, and then it clearly lifted to point toward the forest.

They all followed where it indicated, stepping past brush and over a fallen trunk, until they finally saw an unclothed human body lying among some bushes.

"Braelok!" Madden said, running with Knya to where Braelok lay still. Torque flew above. Hope and anxiety swirled through each one of them while Knya poured some water from her pouch into her hands and rubbed it over Braelok's face. When he didn't stir she gave him a shake.

"Braelok!" she chirped. At that Braelok sprang up from his waist, breathing heavily. Cheers erupted from his three friends.

Knya began laughing and crying at the same time. "We thought you might have been dead," she said.

"Well you might have just given me a heart attack, but I think I'll live." Braelok managed a smile. Then he paused as he saw Madden. His eyes widened looking upon the unicorn boy in his human form, seeing him as he truly was for the first time. Braelok smiled again.

Knya cut a large piece from the bottom of her cape so

Braelok and Madden could share it.

Madden stepped close to Braelok and helped him to his feet. When Braelok was steady they embraced. Their eyes fixed on each other's for a few seconds before both boys looked aside.

"Well, look at this guy," Braelok said. "No more walking on four legs for you, eh?"

"Yeah, you either, I guess," Madden replied.

Knya approached with a bit more caution. "That wasn't you... right?" She looked him over as he lowered his eyes.

"I can't undo what happened when I was under those spells... but I can tell you I wasn't in control. What I told you around the fire on the beach that night was true. My family was taken into slavery. But after months in the confines of the prison camp, *he* appeared where my sister and I slept behind a locked gate.

"In his disguise, he melted the bars away and gave us what we thought was freedom, only to enslave us himself in time. Then I saw him bewitch her. She was touched and... corrupted by evil, by that darkness. I knew he must have intended to do the same to me, although I had no idea how bad it really was. She was no longer my sister, and I was becoming something else too.

"Then one day I saw him working the magick. I knew he was sending them out for another hunt through one of his dark passages. So I jumped through too. I escaped with plans to free her as soon as I could. I ended up on the island and a few days later I came upon you in the forest, being hunted by the same enemy that I had been running from and so badly

188

wanted revenge upon. I had to help you. And you have helped me even more. You have all set me free. And my sister..." Braelok took a deep breath. "She came to me... and told me that you set her free too." As he spoke, his eyes welled up with tears. "I didn't know if I'd ever be able to free her. And when he found me again, I thought I'd never be free myself. I am in debt to you. And I care about you all."

Madden looked to Knya and then to Torque. "Then come with us?" he said, turning to face Braelok.

Braelok smiled at him and then looked at Knya and Torque for their approval. They both smiled.

"I will come with you... if you'll have me," Braelok answered.

"Then let's get going," Knya said. She held out his sword and Braelok accepted it.

"Yes, it is time we headed home," Torque said.

"Home..." Madden looked at his companions and he felt blessed, but thoughts of his family made him realize he longed to see them.

Madden turned back and peered over the ruins of the temple. The events still weighed heavily on him, but he knew how he should try to see things. They had been victorious, but they had endured great peril. And although Madden hadn't made his wish aloud, his heart's desires had come true. He had experienced something marvelous and helped all the people of earth along the way. He turned again to join his friends.

"Madden, help me make the passage?" Knya said.

"Yeah," he said.

Knya lifted her arms, holding the beetle totem in one

hand and made a few outlines in the air with the other. She then began an incantation in English this time. "Return us now from where we came, back to Eloria our will be made." Her gem sparked. Madden joined in and the spot on his forehead began to shine. A stream of colorful light formed in front of them, and they saw the fortress of Eloria in the distance through it.

"Now," Knya said.

Torque flew though, followed by Braelok.

"Go ahead, but keep your focus. I'll follow you," she said to Madden, and he stepped through, doing as she told him.

When Madden emerged on the other side he turned to face the glowing passage. Its light seemed to be fading and Knya was still on the other side. He closed his eyes and focused hard on his intent. The passage glowed brighter and widened, and Knya finally emerged. They had made it back. They all sighed with relief and hoped it was the last time they would do so for a long while.

When they arrived at the fortress, Omnicus and the sorcerers celebrated their return and triumph. All were surprised at meeting Madden in his restored human form. Omnicus opened his large elephant arms and brought Madden in for a long overdue hug now that the boy could reciprocate such a maneuver.

"Glory to you, boy. Glory to all of you!" Omnicus said.

A great feast of sautéed jackfruit, candied yams, curried nuts, seasoned beets and sweet fruit pies was prepared for everyone to enjoy. Knya, Madden, Braelok and Torque ate heartily, reveling in the decadence of flavors. A variety of music played on an old phonograph that seemed to have an enhanced audio power, which sounded very high definition and crisp, as if the musicians of each record were present in the room. Omnicus apparently had a thing for instrumental jazz, but there were several other genres in the rotation, even one Earth, Wind and Fire song.

After dinner, they moved to the yard, where Omnicus and the sorcerers treated the conquering heroes to a visual spectacle of magickal fireworks greater than any of them had ever observed. Across the night sky exploded waves of rainbows, kaleidoscopes of vibrantly lit colors, luminescent shapes of centaurs, merpeople, giraffes, and elephants, and a finale of a unicorn, a dragosaur and two humans together. The illuminations gleamed in all of their eyes and made everyone smile with delight. Braelok put his arm around Madden and pulled him closer. Their eyes connected for a moment before Madden turned his head, his face flushing, but his smile grew even bigger.

As the night grew later and yawns began to sneak out, they all returned inside and began preparing for bed. A few grabbed another slice of fruit pie to help them off before retiring. Then they all said their goodnights and turned in to their quarters.

Madden's large bed felt even larger now that he was a boy again. He tossed for a while before standing, walking to the window and pushing it open. He looked out at the moon and the light that it cast over the mountains of the island. The sight was magnificent but his mind wouldn't settle. Madden truly loved his new family and enjoyed being a unicorn, but after all he had witnessed he knew it was time to go home and see that his first family was safe. He wondered if his mother was worried to illness, imagining something awful had happened to him. He missed all of his family, even his brother, Martin, although if Martin tried to exert the upper hand in any brotherly debates they might have in the future, Madden had a new tactic for settling such things.

And then there was the question of Braelok. Madden wasn't sure if he was interpreting Braelok's kindness in the correct way, or if he was just inflating his own feelings. Madden was finally beginning to understand himself, but that didn't mean what he felt was mutual, even if there had been some display of affection. He was way too apprehensive to consider talking about it, and thought that unless Braelok did, it would go unanswered. He began to feel foolish that a boy like Braelok could ever feel the same way about him. His mind was returning to its previous human deprecation and he stopped it immediately. *One day, when the time is right, I will find someone who sees me as I want to be seen*, he thought.

Then a soft rapping came at his door. Madden's heart jumped as his thoughts projected the prospect of who it might be on the other side. But he let out a breath and laughed at his silly idea as he went to answer.

Madden turned the latch and pulled the door open, and there was Braelok, standing in the moonlit threshold. "I couldn't sleep. I thought I might not be the only one," Braelok said.

Madden, speechless, rapt with surprise and excitement, shook his head.

"Should we take a walk then?" Braelok suggested.

Madden nodded. "Sure," he said, hoping his elevated pulse wasn't completely obvious.

The boys crept quietly through the stone halls, passing the dining area and the main great hall until they crossed out onto the walkways of the gazebo and yard. The night was softly lit with moon and starlight descending upon them, casting a subtle glisten about everything that surrounded them as they sauntered the perimeter. To Madden, Braelok appeared relaxed and he made an effort to do the same as they appreciated the grounds under the delicate glittering above. Toward a far corner of the yard a colorful glow, distinguished from the soft pale light of the night sky, flickered ahead of them between gently windswept draping branches. Remembering the Burning Passion Flowers under the willow tree, they decided to have a closer look, stepping through the scrim of hanging leafy limbs.

Just as Knya had told them, the flowers were glowing brightly casting colorful tones under the canopy of the willow tree. Both of their faces lit as they entered, smiling at one another before closely surveying the glowing blossoms.

"She wasn't lying," Braelok beamed.

"Yeah, no kidding," Madden agreed. In the night's light, the intricate details of the flowers' structures could be observed in unique luminescent hues. The tiny veins of the flowers stood out against the filament of the petals' patterns, which were different shades than the stigma and pollen. Madden leaned close to a bloom to get a scent, and as he inhaled, the flower's luminosity brightened. Both boys gaped and grinned. Braelok leaned in to get a scent too and the flower brightened the same. The boys laughed, turning to each other. Then Braelok took a breath and slowly lifted his hand, moving it toward the hand of the boy who stood before him. Braelok's fingers opened and clasped softly around Madden's.

Madden looked down to where their skin met. It was no accident. Braelok looked into Madden's eyes and smiled. Madden met his gaze, heart fluttering before shying away. But he couldn't stay away from the depth of the russet-umber gemstone eyes that were welcoming him, asking him to see inside, to finally have a real thorough look at them.

They smiled as they peered at one another, into a new world of dimension they had never been immersed in before. Both pairs of hands met, grasping tighter as the sensations of every tiny groove of adjoining skin radiated, filling the boys with want and joy. Their bodies surged with the feeling of finally receiving the unfamiliar touch they had longed for, dreamed of and never believed might be a possibility, surface to surface, but emanating deeply, alive and warm perfectly imperfect contours, rough and soft, and desiring the other's in return.

Braelok pushed Madden's hair from his eyes, revealing the small raised colorless spot where his horn had been. Braelok brushed his finger over it and smiled at Madden again. Madden smiled again too. They couldn't help it, and they didn't want to. The light around them swelled and they realized the glow of the flowers was pulsing softly, seeming to reflect the boys' radiant experience. The extraordinarily lit setting was more than perfect for the occasion.

They remained in the glow of the flowers under the willow tree for a few more moments before they continued along, hand in hand. As they made their way back toward the castle, they stopped at the fountain and sat on its ledge next to one another.

"What will you do... now that you've finished what you were brought here for?" Braelok asked.

Madden shrugged. "I'm sure my family is worried sick. I should make sure they're okay sooner than later, and I miss them a lot. After that, who knows? Going back to my old life feels like a weird thing to do, considering all we've seen and been through, but that's at least where I have to start," Madden said. "What about you? Off to find your mother?"

Braelok nodded. "Yeah," he said.

"That seems like a lot to do alone. You shouldn't have to..."

"We've all got responsibilities. After everything you just had to do, you deserve to have some time with your family. Not to mention they probably are worried sick. I'll be fine," Braelok said. Madden sighed and put his head on Braelok's shoulder. They stayed silent while they watched the twinkling gems above them in the night sky.

After another half an hour had passed, lost in the haze of one another, they decided it best to try and get at least some sleep before morning arrived. They slunk back through the fortress halls, up to the wing of their bed quarters. Braelok insisted on walking Madden to his door and as they said goodnight Braelok pulled Madden close and put his arms around him. Again, the surge passed between them as they embraced, and it was difficult to relinquish. Minutes went by and at last Madden looked up to be sure he wasn't fabricating all of this, but his senses still showed the handsome Braelok in his arms. They finally managed to part, and Madden stepped inside his room.

"Good night," Madden said.

"Sweet dreams," Braelok replied.

Madden hesitantly pushed the door until it closed, watching Braelok until he could no longer see him. He turned and rested his back on the hard surface, breathing deeply, questioning everything he had just experienced, and relishing it all.

Braelok sighed and smiled as he quietly walked back to his own room, stepping inside. Both boys fell asleep in a fog of euphoria.

Madden opened his eyes as he heard bustling in the kitchen. Slivers of sunlight beamed through his window, indicating another beautiful day on the islands of Mythras. Remembering the night with Braelok made his heart thud through his whole body, and he couldn't fight the grin that grew on his face, but it didn't last. Even when taking into account the incredible events of the past few days, this magick was in a class of its own. And now that he had experienced a tiny bit of it, he was sure he had to leave it behind.

The conflict sat in his mind as he pondered and hoped for the possibilities, but he knew that, at least for the time being, they were going in separate directions. He tried to put any sadness out of his mind and concentrate on the joy, and then he stretched and rolled out of bed.

He and Braelok had roused from their rooms at nearly synchronized times, finding each other in the hall when they emerged. They both smirked as they met.

"Morning," Madden said.

"Good morning. Sleep okay?" Braelok asked.

"Great. You?"

"Absolutely."

They wandered toward the lively sounds of breakfast being enjoyed by their companions, and just before they arrived Madden halted, searching for the right words and the courage to say them.

"With all of this, even all the magick... last night might have been the best," Madden said.

Braelok smiled. "Definitely the best for me."

"But... I have to go home."

"I know."

"And you've got your own business to handle. I wish I could come with you, and maybe we can..."

Braelok gently placed his hand behind Madden's head. "Hey, it's okay. We'll find each other again."

Madden nodded as he felt his heart sink, falling into an ache.

In the dining room Knya, Torque, Andun, Ranalin, Omnicus and Meirvot were already enjoying breakfast. Zhao had left Eloria earlier in the morning, but gave his further regards to be conveyed to Madden and Braelok.

The last meal they all shared was a pleasant one, and when it was through Madden reluctantly spoke on the subject that they all knew was coming. "I don't want to leave this place. What will I do without you?" He looked to his companions around the table.

After a pause, Omnicus answered. "You will have adventures of your own, until we meet again, hmm hmm."

"I think it's time, if you can help me return," Madden said.

"You needed but to ask," Omnicus replied.

Bittersweet emotions loomed as they walked through the castle, toward the great hall. Madden took in the last sights of the wondrous place to which he had been called.

When they reached the great hall, Omnicus hugged him warmly. "Here you stand before me as the same soul that I met on that first day, yet you have grown so much because of your own choices to stand in the face of adversity, protect those in need, and open yourself to the possibilities of knowledge beyond, which you now possess. For a human so young, or any creature of any age, you have truly done marvelous things. And the world is better for it. I hope you know this and will take it with you to cherish, hmm hmm. I know you cannot stay, but you are always welcome in Eloria. I do hope you will come back to visit us. I have a feeling you may, when the time is right...and these will help you." Omnicus handed Madden a small vial and an ancient looking hardcover book titled *The History and Practical Applications of the Magickal Arts.* "Within this book is material for the further study of what you have already begun. I think the understanding will come to you without much trouble, hmm. And upon receiving a few rare herbs from Zhao, I was able to concoct this mixture. When you desire, spread this liquid completely around the perimeter of a doorway or threshold and, until it evaporates, Eloria shall await you on the other side."

Madden hugged Omnicus tightly again. "Thank you. This has been greater than any dream I could have imagined. I don't want to wake up, but I guess I've been awake this whole time. After everything, I'm a little afraid to go home. I'm not like the people back home anymore, although I suppose I never really was. But I'm afraid of losing any of this too. I'm afraid of being away from all of you. I couldn't have done any of this, learned any of this, made it through any of this without all of you. I love you all." Madden said, fighting back heavy emotions.

He turned to Knya, and they embraced as Torque flew over to join them.

"We love you, and we'll miss you... so much. And it's not goodbye for good. Please come back before long. How else will I manage around them without you?" Knya said, smiling, holding her own emotions at bay.

"Okay, I promise," Madden said with a tearful chuckle.

"It has been a pleasure and a privilege, young man," Torque said, "don't keep yourself away for too extended of a duration."

"Yes, sir. The privilege is mine," Madden said.

Ranalin, Andun, Tajre and Meirvot all gave Madden a bow and he returned the gesture.

"Many blessings to you." Andun nodded.

"Godspeed," Ranalin said.

"Take care of yourself," Meirvot added.

"We'll see you again," Tajre said.

"Yes, thank you," Madden replied.

Then he turned to Braelok, and when their eyes met, a tear finally made its way down Madden's cheek. The aching in his heart pressed harder against the walls of his chest until it was painful. They pulled each other close and stayed that way for a few moments. Knya, Torque and Omnicus smirked.

"We'll find each other," Braelok said.

"I can't wait," Madden replied. He handed Braelok a piece of paper with his Florida address and phone number on it. "Just in case."

Looking to Omnicus and Knya, Madden nodded. "I'm ready," he said.

They nodded in return. Knya lifted her arms and Omnicus knelt. Her opalium gem glinted with its purple light and Omnicus's tusks lit with their golden glow. A passage formed in front of Madden and he could vaguely see the wooded area where he had first been transformed. He glanced back to his friends and smiled again. Then he stepped into the glimmering doorway.

15

Where The Heart Is

Madden placed his feet onto the familiar Florida soil. He was back in almost the exact spot where Knya had come through to retrieve him days ago. He looked to the disturbed earth where he had laid as he began to transform. The pain of what the boys had done to him had not been erased but the magick that followed softened the edge. He slid his fingers across his forehead and the raised mark was still there. He chortled to himself and felt grateful.

He looked around the forest and all of it seemed more beautiful than he remembered. Taking a full breath of the fresh new air, he turned to begin walking home.

He wasn't sure exactly what to tell his mother, and after several days of absence there must have been a police report filed for a missing thirteen-year-old boy. He doubted Tyson and any of the other boys would have talked about their incident, so it was all up to him. The woods were large enough to technically get lost in but Madden didn't like the idea of lying.

When he arrived at his doorstep he closed his eyes and breathed deeply. Then he twisted the doorknob and went inside.

His mother was dozed off in the living room chair with the phone in her hand, and Mindy slept on the couch. Fliers with Madden's face on them were strewn about and three cups of half-drunk coffee sat on the table near them.

Madden was thankful at the scene. He was sorry that any of it had to happen, but more than happy to know he was so cared for.

Bracing himself to wake his mother, he had a thought. He quietly made his way to the kitchen, opened the book that Omnicus had given him and skimmed through. Briefly seeing what the book offered excited him thoroughly, and after a few minutes he found something that he decided might help him in his current situation. "The Tranquil Mind" was a spell listed among many others, and Madden began reading it meticulously.

Luckily, the spell was not that difficult and had very few steps and ingredients. It called for a choice of several fragrant flowers, tracing a rune in the air with his hand, and an incantation.

Madden tiptoed out to his back yard and plucked some blooming jasmine that had wrapped itself along the fence. Flowers in hand, he returned to his kitchen and began speaking the words of the spell.

"With this sweet aroma, let your mind be soothed. Leave burdened thoughts, by my will subdued." As Madden made the symbol of the rune and repeated the verse, the spot on his forehead twinkled, and then the flowers too began to shimmer. It was working.

He crept back to his mother's side and held the jasmine under her nose, letting her breath in the fragrant scent. After a few moments of normal breathing she took in a noticeably larger breath, and let out a serene sigh while wearing a visible smile.

Madden woke her gently and she slowly opened her eyes. When she saw him she gasped and pulled him into her arms tightly. Tears ran down her face. "Oh, Madden. I was so worried," she said. The spell had worked to calm her, but there was almost no magick that was a match for a mother's love.

"Madden!" Mindy woke and attacked him with a gripping hug of her own.

They held him for several minutes before his mother asked where he had been, and what had happened.

Madden found the words to tell her the truth, even if he left out some details. "I was making my way through the woods... and all of a sudden I didn't recognize anything. But after a few days I found my way home. I'm so sorry, mom."

She hugged him snugly again and insisted he come into the kitchen to eat something. He didn't argue or let on that he had just eaten plenty only an hour or so prior.

Martin arrived home as Madden finished his sandwich. He stopped when he saw Madden and sighed with relief. He hugged his brother heartily, and then shook his head as he faked a chin punch. Madden smiled. Martin questioned his disappearance too, and Madden gave the same answer he had before, all the while a bit of fragrant jasmine flower sat on the counter near him. Madden was happy to be home.

The fliers that declared him missing were taken down and the police were satisfied with the account of his time away. Going back to school was the last hurdle to cross.

Madden wore his bangs a little lower than usual when he returned to Washington Middle School. The halls felt strange to be surrounded by again— the bustling sea of students hurrying to classes before an audio tone might mark their tardiness and repercussions would ensue, the restraints against the simple freedom to use the restroom at one's own need, unless with permission and pass, the pecking order of peers, all the careful worry he had felt on a daily basis—it all seemed insignificant and a bit silly now. He held knowledge and education in the highest regard, but the means by which it was conducted felt odd. Although he thought it could use some changes, he laughed it off and played the game.

Upon reuniting with Sienna, she hugged him so tightly he thought she might break his shoulder, but he was more than glad to see her too. Other than the normal questioning of his disappearance, they picked up almost exactly where they left off, as good friends do.

The day began to feel less surreal as it passed, and Madden began to settle back into the idea of having at least a partly normal life. He actually didn't mind a bit of structured quaint simplicity after the frightening side of possibilities he had witnessed in the previous days. He thought to himself that he would continue to use his power for good. There were plenty of things in everyday life that could use some positive magick.

As the last bell rang to dismiss the day, Madden gathered his books and made his way out of his history class.

"Glad you're back with us, Mr. Edwards," his teacher, Mr. Jotson, said to him.

"Thank you, sir. Me too," Madden said.

His old routine would have been to hurry away from the school as quickly as he could to avoid any trouble, but today he took his time. He walked to his locker and deposited a few books and then headed down the hall, weaving through other students, toward the school exit. He stepped into the sunshine and inhaled the fresh air that floated on a gentle wind.

He began on his way home when he saw Tyson Oliver standing under a tree in the schoolyard along with the other boys that had chased and assaulted him in the forest. He hesitated for a moment but reminded himself that no one would ever believe them if they did tell anyone about what they saw, and it was they who should feel shameful about what they did. He himself had value and worth, with or without magick.

Madden held his head high and continued walking. When the boys saw him, Madden paid them no mind. To his relief, after noticing him, they all turned to look away—all except one of Tyson's friends who was absent from the chase into the woods and hadn't witnessed the events that followed.

"Watch out guys, queer coming through. If it comes any closer we have the right to kick its teeth in," the boy said as Madden passed them. The boy seemed surprised when Tyson and the others didn't chime in at all.

Madden stopped walking. He knew he should try to ignore him, but he decided this harassment was going to have to stop, for all of the students' sakes. Madden turned to face the boy.

"Oh no, if they look at you, do you get infected?" The boy looked away and laughed.

Then Madden's gaze tilted up toward the tree boughs. Madden concentrated and the spot on his forehead glowed dimly under the hair that covered it. A second later a thin dead branch fell from the tree and latched around the boy like a grappling hand, eliciting him to squeal out a high-pitched sound that made everyone in the yard turn. Laughter erupted from all around as twigs flew, while the boy thrashed to free himself. Madden couldn't help but smile. Tyson and all of his friends gaped at Madden.

"Let's try to get along this year, guys. Cool?" Madden asked. He didn't wait for a response.

"Madden!" Sienna called across the yard and Madden went to join her. They laughed and walked home at an untroubled pace.

As Madden lay in bed after his first day back at school, he read through a dense chapter on the history of magick in the book Omnicus had given him and closed it when he had finished. He felt the distance between himself and his friends in Eloria was at its greatest. His time in Eloria was still so fresh in his mind and yet he was now so far away. He stored the traveling potion that he was given in a safe place and vowed only to use it when he was sure he could afford the time, and no one would be worried about him. He had already caused enough commotion in town, but he missed his new friends dearly. Visions of Braelok made his body ache and he began to feel melancholy at the thought of losing what they had shared.

A soft knock came at his slightly opened bedroom door, pulling him from his thoughts. His mother poked her head in, and Mindy's followed.

"Goodnight, sweetie," his mom said. "I love you."

"I love you too, mom," he replied. She kissed him on his head.

"I'm glad you're not lost anymore." Mindy hugged him.

"Thanks, kiddo," Madden said.

His mother and Mindy left the room as Martin entered, plopping into his own bed. "Goodnight, dork," Martin said.

"Goodnight, Ogre," Madden countered.

Madden smiled and tried to relax. He had so much to be happy about, and he promised that he would see his friends again. But for now, he would enjoy the blessings of where he was. And tomorrow morning, when the sun rose again, he would do all that he could to be helpful, hopeful, kind, strong and marvelous.

ACKNOWLEDGMENTS

I had help with this book so I suppose thanks are in order. To my imaginative and skilled editors: Eliza, Stephen, Sean, Judith and Michele, thank you for helping my story bloom. Hope and Simone, thank you for creating the illustrations of my dreams. To Tim, thank you for your help with this book and your dedication to nurturing the arts. And to my wonderful family who have always given me tremendous love. You have been my greatest blessings.

THE AUTHOR

The author is a fantasy/sci-fi/horror super-nerd who also has a love of music and film. She lives in Los Angeles with the most beautiful cat in the world.

For more information, musings and magick check out
ErickaPage.com

A Marvel of Magick :
Madden and The Dark Unicorns of Danuk

Illustrations by Hope Christofferson

Cover Illustration by Simone Torcasio

CPSIA information can be obtained
at www.ICGtesting.com
Printed in the USA
LVHW030158240421
685422LV00004B/172